A Broken River Books original

Broken River Books
10660 SW Murdock St
#PF02
Tigard, OR 97224

ISBN: 978-1-940885-33-9

Printed in the USA.

ZERO SAINTS

A barrio noir

by Gabino Iglesias

BROKEN RIVER BOOKS
PORTLAND, OR

Para Gabi, el niño mágico.

1
Roberto Roena
Stinky trunk – Fucked
La santa y afilada guadaña
Praying – Pupils invaded by darkness
Beheading
Santa Muerte

I didn't hear those pinches cabrones coming. They cracked my skull from behind. Probably expected me to drop like a sack of hammers, but the blow came with too much power and not enough finesse. You can't just whack someone on the head and expect them to go down for good. Some folks have really hard heads. Now I knew mine was, and I had my iPod to blame.

I stumbled and covered up in case there was more coming. No vino nada. That was it. Someone grunted in surprise or frustration, loud enough for me to hear it over the music in my ears. El cencerro de Roberto Roena es mágico.

One hand grabbed my neck and kept me down. Three other hands darted in and crawled over me like nervous cockroaches. They pulled my gun from my waistband, fished my cell phone and keys out of my right pocket, and yanked the earbuds out of my ears.

With my skull unplugged, I heard a car pull up beside me. It purred like a large cat. I twisted my head a bit.

Big.

Blue paint.

Dirty.

Cholo rims reflecting the orange light of a nearby lamppost and six legs, two pairs in shorts and one stuffed in jeans. I wanted to break all of them.

The trunk opened and stayed low like a fat man doing pushups. They shoved me toward the back of the car with my head still down. I thought about taking a swing, trying to crack some huevos. That left two more, surely packing, plus whoever was in the car. Bad math.

The hinges of the trunk screamed like a fried egg under a spatula. The hands pushed me in hard. They slammed it shut.

My right knee cracked. White noise shot up to my brain. The trunk lid bounced back up with a groan that echoed my own. Hija de puta. I tried to curl into a fetal position. Not enough space to pull it off quickly. I hugged my knee and looked up, saw two guys for a second, their faces black masks in the scant light. One wore a white t-shirt. He leaned forward and tried again. With both hands.

SLAM!

It worked. Then, darkness. The car moved forward, but didn't burn rubber.

My heart buzzed. I sucked in huge gulps of warm air. There was not enough oxygen for me in that trunk. My chest couldn't expand properly. I was stuck, trapped, squeezed. Panic bit me. La mala muerte andaba cerca. These pinches mamones caught me slippin'. They had my piece. I was dead. Muerto y sin poder despedirme de mi vieja.

Then I remembered I was in Austin, not Mexico. Folks don't get their heads blown off in the streets in Austin. Bodies aren't hung from bridges or stuffed into suitcases and left on the side of the road. No one gets a box in the mail containing a severed head. Although most politicians deserve it, los narcos don't kidnap them while leaving the office and put two full mags in their brains. Nah, this is a nice, civilized town full of wannabe artists, students, and hipsters. The only thing people fear in this place is getting their tongues burned at their favorite coffee joint. Plus, los cabrones that jumped me were brown. If they wanted me dead, I'd be dead. No hitting or kidnapping bullshit. That's what los blancos do. Con nosotros, it's a bullet to the brain y buenas noches. This was different.

I reminded myself to breathe, pay attention, focus.

I took another breath. It felt like something.

I closed my eyes and started praying to la Santa Muerte, mi divina guardiana, for protection and guidance.

Señora Blanca, Señora Negra, a tus pies me postro para pedirte, para suplicarte, que hagas sentir tu fuerza, tu poder y tu omnipotencia contra los que intenten destruirme.

I felt better, calmer, more aware of everything. I kept going, the familiar words pouring from my mouth and dragging some of the fear out with them.

Señora te imploro seas mi escudo y mi resguardo contra el mal, que tu guadaña protectora corte lo obstáculos que se interpongan, que se abran las puertas cerradas y se muestren los caminos.

The scythe was with me, la santa y afilada guadaña. It would keep other sharp things away from my neck, shield me from bad intentions and danger. Mi Santa Muerte had done it many times before and would do it again now. I had nothing to fear.

Señora mía, no hay mal que tu no puedas vencer ni imposible que no se doble ante tu voluntad, a ella me entrego y espero tu benevolencia...

I could finally take my first real breath. The trunk smelled like an old, rotting sofa. Something hard and pointy was pushing against my lower back. I tried to move, to uncoil a bit, but my shoulders were stuck. The car stopped. Probably a red light. A moment later, the vehicle turned a hard left. I'd parked on the corner of I-35 and 3rd Street. We were going south on Red River.

I breathed again and listened. Something obnoxious was punishing the car's speakers with too much bass. Noise filled the trunk. The back of my head was on fire. A warm worm inched its way down my scalp. Sangre. In my crunched, sideways position, I couldn't touch and check, so I tried to forget about it. My knee was still screaming.

Why was I here?

Between the pain, the discomfort, and the circus music, my brain refused to function properly. I thought hard about the last few weeks, months, but no reasons came. I didn't owe any money. I was dealing from the door of The Jackalope, on 6th Street, and that was well within Zetas territory. To my knowledge, I hadn't banged anyone's girl.

It didn't take long.

The car kept going, turning left and right way too many times for me to keep track or try to guess our destination. A few minutes later, we slowed down, stopped. The driver jerked the parking brake. Engine and awful music died simultaneously. My chest wanted to implode, swallow me, help me disappear. Del polvo venimos y al polvo vamos, but the bitch is not being able to become polvo painlessly when you need it most. I was a wounded animal, waiting.

Nothing happened for about half a dozen eternities. Then the car rocked a tad. Doors opened and slammed shut in quick succession. They popped the trunk. It jumped a bit, as if sick of being pressed against me. El sentimiento era mutuo. Then the banshee screamed. It was dark, but a lamppost half a block away threw some of what it had to offer our way, bathing us in yellowish light. Three goons stood there side by side, looking down at me. I looked back. Vestimenta de tipo duro que escucha mucho hip hop. Lots of ink. Heads thrown back, necks spread like angry cobras. They wanted to look menacing and were pulling it off. Two held guns. The guy on the left aimed his at my face. A black thing. Blocky. Looked like a 9mm in the dark. Ready to spit death. He held it sideways, like every pendejo who's more worried about looking tough than hitting his target. The guy in the middle let his piece hang loosely by his side. He was the one rocking the jeans. Both cabrones looked comfortable with the situation. That made me uncomfortable.

Mr. Jeans brought his head down. His neck deflated. The shadows covering his face became ink. Tenia la cara cubierta de tatuajes. Seeing the tattoos was worse than spotting the guns or getting whacked in the head. The blackness covering his features sprouted ghostly tendrils that seeped into the night around us and made everything darker. Impossibly darker.

"Pa' fuera," said he said. His voice carried no inflection or emotion. He'd done this before.

I moved slowly, almost sat up. My knee wasn't cooperating much. I slid out of the trunk with the grace of a newborn giraffe. Mr. Jeans turned sideways to give me some maneuvering space and grabbed my arm. He leaned in like someone would at a bar filled with loud music, even though the street was quiet.

"Now we go in the house...y te quiero calladito, maricón," he said, squeezing my bicep, physically putting the accent on the last syllable of maricón.

He started walking briskly, pulling me along with him, ignoring my limp. I looked around. We were on a residential street. Small houses looking like shit. Dead front lawns. Peeling paint. Cracked sidewalk. Shitty cars. Yellow weeds and brown dirt where there should have been green. There was another goon sitting in the blue boat with the rusty trunk hinges. We were somewhere in East Austin.

One of the other guys closed the trunk behind us. I jumped. It felt like someone had stuck an icicle up my ass and poked my heart with it. Mr. Jeans grabbed me a little tighter, dug his bony fingers into my arm like an angry parent.

We walked up to a small, one-story house with fading blue paint on its walls and climbed two creaky wooden steps to a door. Mr. Jeans opened the door and walked in, pulling me into the dark behind him. The two monkeys followed. Someone flipped a switch. Se hizo la luz y se apagaron mi ojos.

Mr. Jeans let go of my arm. We stood in an empty

living room. My three captors were looking at me, all red eyes, dilated pupils, and macho attitude. I blinked a few times, waiting for my eyes to adjust to the light. I glanced around at darker places. Small kitchen to the right, door to the left, dark hallway straight ahead. I came back to the three cabrones looking at me like I'd banged their mom.

Mr. Jeans had the most ink covering his features. I couldn't make most of it out, a complicated mess of lines, signs, letters, numbers, and blotchy shit obviously done by a twitchy preso with a guitar string and more free time than skills. However, I could make out a 13 right above a hand making the devil horns on his neck and the letters MS covering a chunk of his forehead and left eye. Mara Salvatrucha. Fear gripped the back of my head so hard I stopped feeling the pain in my knee. La Salvatrucha le da pesadillas al Diablo. El Cartel de Sinaloa sometimes hires mareros to do the dirty work. I thought about my sister and felt death creeping up on me again. No me falles, Santa Muerte. I closed my eyes, pictured mi Santísima Muerte sitting on her altar at home, tried to feel her strength around me.

"We gonna go see Indio now. You no say nothing, hijueputa. You listen to him. I see you no pay attention… te haces el bravo, lo que sea, te meto una bala entre las cejas."

His English was fucking atrocious. My guess is he kept using it for the same reason all new immigrants keep at it: he wanted to blend in. With a face full of ink, buena suerte con eso, huevón.

He used the gun to signal toward the hallway. The only guy who hadn't shown me his gun was already heading that way. I followed him.

There was a door on the left at the end of the hallway, a thin line of light underneath it. Mr. No Gun opened the door, looked back, stood aside, nodded me in.

The room was small, the air thick with an acrid mix of weed smoke, sweat, and stale piss. Un tipo flaco sin camisa with coppery skin covered in tattoos stood next to a chair. He was holding a large knife with nasty teeth. Como el que usaba mi abuela para cortar el pan. His black pants were too short to be long and too long to be shorts. The shoes on his feet looked five sizes too big and they were vomiting their tongues like alley winos. He wore no socks. Surely that contributed to the smell in the room. His gun was tucked in the front. It had gold grips. I thought about grabbing the piece and shooting his huevos off and, for the first time in a long while, I almost laughed. Seeing the man in the chair stopped me.

His head was down, his arms and legs taped to the armrests and legs of the chair with duct tape. His hands had gone white from lack of circulation. Blood and saliva were mixing with the sweat that covered his chest and belly. They'd obviously worked him over for a while. He wore blue boxer shorts and nothing else. He'd pissed himself at some point. Next to the chair was a large white bucket. There was nothing else in the room. Los tipos no estaban ahí para quedarse. Mala señal.

Indio smiled, grabbed the dude on the chair by the hair and yanked back. A bloated, bruised version of Nestor Torres' face came up. The left side looked a tad rough, but the right one looked like he had tried to get a kiss from a moving freight train. His eyes were in another dimension, showing more white than anything else. Whatever they'd given him had him flying somewhere between unconsciousness and outer space. A silver leach of snot coated his upper lip. His mouth hung open, drooling a gooey combination of saliva and blood onto his chest. I couldn't spot any teeth in there. I was pregnant with fear, pero el pobre Nestor estaba peor que yo, ya estaba jodido.

"We asked little Nestor here to give your jefe a message," said Indio. "He asked us who the fuck we were to be sending messages. So we showed him. Creo que ya lo esta entendiendo. Now I want to show you."

Indio reached down and grabbed the index finger of Nestor's right hand. He pulled it, placed the knife near the knuckle, and used it as a saw. He threw his entire skinny body into it, lifting himself on tiptoes to apply pressure. Two moves was all it took. The cartilage didn't put up too much of a fight. Nestor tensed up a bit and scrunched up his face, but no sound came from his destroyed mouth. Indio held up the severed finger to make sure I got a good look at it and then threw it in the bucket. El dedo hit the inside of the bucket and then the bottom. Thud, thud. The two thuds were almost worse than the cutting. Then a loud crunch came from inside the bucket. It was followed by a second crunch.

Indio looked at me, pointed at my face with the bloody utensil. "Tell your jefe la Salvatrucha didn't come here to play. We want to run things downtown entre I-35 y Mopac, de la MLK hasta el río. El resto es suyo. Sus mierdas de vendedores se pueden quedar si quieren, pero trabajando para nosotros. He can have the east side y todo al norte de la universidad. We supply everything and take un poquito de lo que se embolsilla. If his supplier in Dallas tiene un problema con eso, we can fix it real quick. Is a good deal, no?"

What he was offering was preposterous. Guillermo would never give up downtown because more than half his business, at least the business that mattered, came from there. From musicians to workers and from college students to homeless junkies, downtown Austin is where folks go to get drugs. However, I wasn't about to tell crazy Indio with the huge knife what I thought. Besides not wanting him to get angry and turn the instrument on me, I was also sure that, if I dared speak, my voice would come out resembling the sound that would come out of a pigeon's throat right before a cat bites down on it. I kept my mouth shut and nodded.

"What, you're not gonna say anything? You gonna take mi mensaje al gordo de tu jefe just like that? If you do, he'll ignore it. Sabes por que? Because your jefe es un pendejo y los Zetas lo tiene cogido por los huevos. He likes easy money and hates risks. He's nothing but a fat cat that's used to being in the sofa all day long. Por eso el negocio no es mas grande en esta ciudad llena de dinero. If he knew how to run things, he'd be nadando en plata. We're different. We don't mind getting dirty. We know how to run things. We know… como convencer a las personas de que cooperen con nosotros, just like your friend Nestor here. Isn't that right, amigo?"

Indio reached down, grabbed Nestor's middle finger, and repeated the process. This time, the finger came off after a single, brutal stroke. There was almost no blood. A low, guttural growl came from Nestor's mouth. It was drowned in fluids and sounded like something from beyond the grave. Then his head came down again and he passed out, all his tensed muscles suddenly deflating. Indio threw the finger in the bucket again. Only one thud this time. Then came the crunch again.

"You think I'm fucking around, puto?" Indio grabbed Nestor's ring finger and once again applied the knife. He didn't even bother to throw the finger in the bucket before grabbing the pinky and cutting it off as well. Cartilage and pieces of bone dangled at the tip of Nestor's stumps like maggots.

My heart was trying to climb its way out of my chest. It was trapped in my throat. Indio took four steps and grabbed my face. I wanted to kill him, but was too scared to move, too terrified to utter a single word. If you talk to enough men about danger, you'll learn they always overcome their cowardice and triumph. Bullshit. Yo soy un cobarde que disfruta estar vivo y quiero seguir estándolo a toda costa. Keeping your mouth shut and nodding is a good way to stay alive.

"Ya te lo dije, cabrón, no estamos jugando." Indio's breath was as bad as his intentions. I wanted to move back, but my body was locked in place, my eyes bouncing from one of his dilated pupils to the other, waiting for la huesuda to pop out of them any second.

"You should go and talk to your jefe, tell him what you saw, and convince him to make this a smooth transition. Esa sería la opción inteligente. La segunda opción es ponerte bruto. You can go and try to warn him, get everyone riled up and coming for us. Esa sería una movida muy estúpida. We don't want to work too hard for this, chulo, but we will if we have to. We don't mind a little blood."

Indio let go of my face and turned around. His back was entirely covered with black ink: a naked woman, a devil with a smile on his face, a few guns, and a lot of random images I couldn't make out. Indio took two steps forward, reached the chair, and grabbed Nestor's hair. He yanked his head to the left and placed the bloody knife on his neck and looked back at me. His eyes looked dirty, wrong, like the ink on his face had somehow invaded his capillaries. He looked back at Nestor and started sawing at his neck like it was nothing.

Nestor tensed, hummed a high-pitched noise somewhere between a scream and a machine about to give out. Instead of spurts, Nestor's blood came out like a small, fast tide. It soon covered his left side with shiny darkness. Indio started talking gibberish.

"Ogún oko dara obaniché aguanile ichegún iré."

With each word, my core temperature dropped a few degrees. Nestor, thankfully, relaxed. He was gone. Indio kept cutting. When he hit the spinal cord, he let go of Nestor's hair and used that hand to smack the head. There was a loud crack. I closed my eyes, but still heard a few seconds of cutting and then the head hitting the ground.

"Abre los ojos, marica," said Indio. I obeyed.

Indio was pointing at me with the knife. He smiled and dropped the bloody blade on the floor.

"You go and talk to you boss. If I have to bring you here again, te voy a cortar la cabeza. I don't think you want to end up like your friend here, so make sure my message reaches el gordo."

Many bad experiences in Mexico had given me the ability to be in a moment but hover above it so that everything looked like it was happening to someone else. I was barely pulling that shit off this time around. My prayers became a jumble of words that trampled each other in the haste to get out and protect me.

Santa Muerte, protégeme.

That was all I could think about, the only prayer, an improvised mantra.

Santa Muerte, protégeme.

Santa Muerte, protégeme.

I kept repeating as if the words themselves could carry me away from that place, as if they could fly in like avenging angels, lift me by the arms, and fly me to a safe place.

Santa Muerte, protégeme. Por favor, te lo ruego.

One of the goons pulled me by the arm, mumbled something. Vámonos era una de las palabras. It sounded like the best idea anyone had ever had. This culero was no angel, but he was as good as one if he was taking me out of there. I turned without looking at Nestor again.

I shambled down the hall and out of the house.

They pushed me into the car and I kind of wished they'd stuffed me in the trunk again so I could pray in peace, say thank you, cry. Instead, I was squeezed between two guys, their body heat pressing against me like a solid object. The one on the left pulled out a red bandana from his pocket, tied it sloppily around my head. I kept my mouth shut. So did they. I did my best to hide in that silence.

The ride seemed to go on forever. When they removed the bandanna, we were parked behind my car. The guy on my right opened his door, slid out. I waited, fearing they'd shoot me in the back the second I stepped out.

"Pa' fuera, marica," he said.

Somehow those words gave me the strength to get out. The guy outside threw my keys and my phone near my car, lifted a finger, looked ready to say something. He said nothing. I got the message. He got back in the car and they drove away. I stood there, scared, thankful.

Nestor's ghost was gonna be hard to shake.

I walked up to my car, picked up the keys with a hand that shook like a palm tree in a hurricane. Then, a welcome touch of anger. Los hijos de puta nunca me devolvieron mi pistola y mi iPod.

2

La frontera
Death in a bathroom – Amigos
Bones in the desert – El Coyote
Estados Desunidos
Sleeping pills

What happens when someone makes you look at the business end of a gun is that it stirs up everything you think you know. It breaks things, shifts ideas around that you'd previously considered unmovable.

Todo deja de ser roca para convertirse en agua. Everything flows. Everything acquires the consistency of shadows seen in dreams.

When someone shows you the perfectly round, pupil-less black eye of oblivion, you start thinking about what got you there. You start digging around your past looking for the decisions and mistakes that led to that point. Es lo mismo cuando te intentan romper el craneo. And what happens then, what happens when you get a lump the size of an egg on the back of your skull, whether you want it to or not, is that you start seeing these highlights in your head, something like a short movie of the most relevant moments of your immediate past. If you're the kind of person who ends up with a gun in your face, chances are that movie sucks and you look like a fucking pendejo in it. All bloopers, no highlights.

What happens if you're me is that your little pelicula is a perfect mix of clichés and bad luck. You remember a lot, but none of it is worth remembering.

Yeah, if you're me, everything that has to do with being en los Estados Desunidos starts in a club in DF. El Colmillo. Seedy joint, but only if you go in deep and know the back of it. You know, like a girl with a pretty face y el culo sucio. Well, olvida eso because it actually starts elsewhere, a little earlier, at a house party on a night so hot the air feels and smells like a panting dog's breath after a long run on the beach. You're drunk and horny and craving tamales and high as a fucking seagull trying to get away from a storm. Your cell phone rings. It's your sister. She's in a club, as always. She's your only sibling and you can't help but love her, but she's a slutty junkie who brings you more trouble than smiles. Al carajo eso de los picnics familiares.

So, anyway, what happens is that your phone rings. You see ISA on the screen in blocky white letters. Short for Isabel. You pick up. She's screaming something about a man grabbing her ass. It's an old story. Her words bring back images of snot running down her face, ruined mascara, and blood on your hands. Many men have grabbed her ass, but this particular one, just like a few other pinches cabrones in the past who have regretted it, did so without her permission. That makes her angry and her anger makes you angry. It's tu mamá in your head. *Proteje a tu hermana,* she says, her voice coming from nowhere and everywhere at once. *A las chicas hay que cuidarlas,* she repeats for the zillionth time. Familia es familia. You're wired to react, to protect, to lash out and punish al atrevido. The horniness and highness fuel the anger. You tell Javi and Luis to come with you. It's time to teach una lección a un pendejo. You jump in Javi's car and get to the club before the rage in your chest and head has had a chance to burn out, to dissipate like the morning fog.

The gorilla working the door at El Colmillo is mellow as fuck when he sees three dudes with awful intentions approaching. He's used to gringos and chilangos with day jobs looking for a good time, overpriced drinks, and maybe a sweaty encounter in a filthy bathroom stall. He knows the three of you are as far from that demographic as Haiti is from Beverly Hills. No one has to flash un poco de metal to make him step aside and open the door. Dude isn't getting paid enough to take a bullet for this gig.

Your sister is near the bar, standing there with a friend, looking pissed. She points the guy out. You tell her to disappear. You walk over to the asshole, grab him by the shirt, stick your piece into his ribs, tell him to shut the fuck up and walk. You push him toward the bathroom. He threatens you all the way there, says you better let him go or else.

Algunos idiotas no saben seguir instrucciones.

You open the door with his body. The bathroom is packed with sweaty men. Javi and Luis wave their metal around and clear the place in five seconds. No one complains or tries to finish their business. It's the chilango way: when shit goes south, run away and forget what you saw.

The first time you bring the butt of the gun down on the dude's mouth coincides with the bathroom door opening.

Two teeth crack.

One punch flies.

The ass-grabber goes down. So does Javi. You turn to find Luis aiming at three guys. Javi's kneeling, hands cradling his face. Shit's gone sour quick. Who the hell are these guys? The guy you're holding keeps saying you have no idea who you're fucking with. He's right.

Everyone plays tough, but no one wants to die, so the ass-grabber reaching for his piece surprises you. It almost surprises you more than your finger tightening on the trigger.

Boom.

The bathroom fills up with the sound. Suddenly all you hear is a howling wind that's not really there, like a lobo in the desert that's too close for comfort. The smell of cordite covers the stench of ammonia. Bloody Mouth goes down, doesn't even twitch once. Luis reacts, pops two guys fast. The sound of the shots reaches your ears through a few feet of cotton and wet towels. The third guy nails Luis in the gut, bending him over and making him scream like an angry tiger. Javi gets the shooter in the chest while still kneeling. You watch the asshole go down hard. Luis is not moving. Javi yanks you out of there and you're gone through the back door before the bathroom door closes.

The four minutes that follow play around with the fabric of time. The high is long gone, the anger replaced by fear.

Lights.

Clumsy speed.

Your heart thrumming in your throat.

Panic squeezing your ribcage.

Santa Muerte, si salgo de esta, te compro una botella de ron.

Santa Muerte, protégeme ahora como me has protegido siempre.

Santa Muerte, a ti me encomiendo.

Santa Muerte, bendita Santa Muerte, protégeme.

As always, la Santa Muerte gets you home in one peace. You owe her much more than a bottle of rum. You owe her everything. Again.

Then comes the silence, pregnant with bad possibilities, and the nerves. You spend long hours pacing, thinking, regretting. You wait. The doubts invade your blood and pull las pesadillas al lado de los despiertos. You stay inside, talk to no one, send Javi a text telling him to do the same. Time goes by too damn slowly or too damn fast, but it never feels right.

Two days later Luis dies in the hospital. Your sister calls to tell you. She's in Monterey with a friend, but knows a guy who works at Hospital General de Balbuena. She tells you Luis was unconscious when he arrived and stayed that way. That's good because unconscious people don't talk to the cops. The rest is bad. Fucking terrible. You cry. You cry because he's dead and you loved him. You cry because you asked him to go with you. You cry because you left him there, gutshot on a fucking dirty bathroom floor.

You stay inside, wondering, torn between the conflicting theories in your head.

The guy was no one.

The guy had to be someone.

You're fine, you can leave the house, show your face around.

If you leave the house, estás muerto…

Two more days go by. Sleep deprivation has you jumping at the sound of the toilet flushing. You're sure the cat's neighbor is a demon who screams your whereabouts into the dark night so it'll carry in the wind and reach the ears of those who might be looking for you. There's a black hole in the center of your stomach that aches all the time, doesn't let you eat, doesn't let you think. Javi calls, says the whole thing probably died with Luis. He's slurring his words, his drunken mouth too damn close to the phone. He invites you to go drown your sorrows with him at a titty bar. You tell him to stay inside. You say this with one hand holding the phone and the other holding your gun. He chuckles into your ear. The sound is out of place and ugly, like a glass shattering against a wall in the middle of the night. You can tell his laugh is full of nerves and things unsaid. You hang up. He goes alone. He drinks for a while at the same place everything went down because that's what a real macho does. Then he gets up to take a piss. Someone introduces his neck to a broken beer bottle nine or ten times. He bleeds to death in a quarter inch of stale piss.

Two friends dead, both of them in a filthy bathroom of DF. Welcome to Mexico, cabrones. The certainty that this will also happen to you fills you with the kind of dread that invades every thought, every breath, every beat of your racing heart.

One of the bartenders at El Colmillo, Israel, was from your barrio, a few years older than you. He used to play with your primos near your house, used to know your abuelos. He knows you used to run around with Javi, so he calls you with the news as soon as he walks into the bathroom and sees the man on the floor, his neck a too-red mess. He also saw the guy who walked into the bathroom after Javi. He puts two and two together. Te rayaste, cabrón, he says. Then he drops some info on you.

The ass-grabber was wasting some fresh money in DF and setting up some deals para el Cartel de Sinaloa. El hijo de puta andaba en territorio de la Federación. You want to reach up and ask for help, ask someone in la Federación to take care of this for you, to protect you, but you're too low on the food chain and no one is going to start whacking Sinaloa people just to keep your worthless ass safe.

The choices are clear: o te vas o te mueres.

Your tio Silvio, your mother's older brother, knows a good coyote, one of the very few who doesn't just drive around Mexico before dropping folks in the back of a building, broke, scared, and blindfolded. Silvio also has a friend in Austin, Texas, who owes him a few favors. Tio Silvio was part of la vieja guardia, he knows things and he's still alive, so when he tells you the best thing to do is disappear before someone comes for you, you do what he says. He tells you where to meet the coyote and you swallow a dozen questions because he sounds angry, so you jot down the address he gives you and thank him quickly before hanging up.

You're still terrified and nervous and looking for someone to give some of your anger to, so you talk to the coyote while squeezing his balls and pushing your gun against his tonsils. Nada de pinches trucos, you tell him. No te pases de listo, huevón, o te va a salir muy caro. He gets the message.

You pack light. A few shirts, some jeans, and your Santa Muerte statue, which is a foot tall and almost too big for your backpack. You slip out late at night and don't tell your vieja you're leaving. You want to be a macho about this, but you're sad and scared and there are tears in your eyes.

The coyote lost his van in a raid and had to borrow one from another coyote. It needs to be cleaned before you guys can get going. The coyote tells you to sit up front. He drives with the windows down and keeps his mouth shut. Los Tigres del Norte come from the speakers and numb your brain with their loud accordion.

Two hours later you're looking at a big hole in the ground somewhere in the Parque Estatal Tiacaque. The coyote opens the back doors and asks you to give him a hand. Stacked in the back of the van are six bodies. Three men, one woman, two kids. A trip gone wrong, he says with a shrug. The bodies are bloated from the heat, the skin on their wrists tight against zip-ties. You gag, tell the coyote to go fuck himself. He says nothing and gets to work. You sit in the car and jump a little every time you hear a body thud against the ground.

The coyote makes one more stop to pick up a quiet old man in Ciudad Victoria and then enters the US through Matamoros with the help of two gringos dressed like they just stepped off a plane from Iraq. The coyote never talks to you while he drives and you like it that way. He never asks for more money to grease palms during the trip and doesn't say he has to leave you in the middle of nowhere. The old man has no idea how lucky he is to be riding with you. He sleeps in the back with his head against the window for most of the trip, snoring so loud he sometimes wakes himself. He gets off almost as soon as you cross the border, says he's meeting someone. You notice then he has no luggage and wonder about his future, but he's out of your head the second the coyote steps on the gas.

A day later, the coyote drops you off in front of a beige building and doesn't say goodbye. You're just glad to be out of the van and away from the norteño music. If you never hear a song again by Los Herederos del Norte, Ramón Ayala, o Los Tigres del Norte, it'll be too damn soon.

A fat man is waiting for you in front of the building. He calls out and waves you over. He looks pissed, in a hurry. He shakes your hand like he's handing you a rotting sardine. Tío Silvio lied. The man owed him small favors. Nada grande. At least that's what you're led to believe based on the way he "sets you up."

You walk behind the man up some cracked stairs and then follow him into a second-floor studio apartment. It's furnished with shit someone threw away and he tells you the shower works when it wants to. The fat man drops a key on top of the table by the door and disappears. He doesn't tell you how to get in touch with him. You're too tired to ask. You set up the Santa Muerte in a corner next to the old bed, say a quick prayer, ignore the sounds coming from your belly, and try to get some sleep.

The second day an old man named Julio shows up and says he and Silvio used to run around together, says that motherfucker always knew where the bodies were hidden and then slaps you on the back while he laughs. You can't bring yourself to join him.

Julio has smart eyes, a white goatee, and a few strands of greasy grey hair tied in a ponytail. He gives you a cup of lukewarm coffee that tastes like dirty water and a couple of cold egg, cheese, and bacon tacos wrapped in aluminum foil. They taste like heaven. Julio tells you he got you a job at a pizza joint called The Mellow Mushroom. "Es un sitio de gringos, pero pagan bien y no hacen preguntas," he says. Then he tells you you'll be washing dishes and offers you a ride if you're ready to get started. You go, hoping it'll help take your mind off other things. He drops you there and hands you a few crumpled dollars and points at a bus stop two blocks down. "You want la número cinco. Count nine stops and then get off. You'll be in front of your building. Same number of stops coming down." He smiles and drives away.

You wash dishes and the water is so hot your arms are peeling by the end of the day.

The third day on the job, you step out back to throw two bags in the dumpster. You have a key hanging from a long piece of wood. It surprises you that the gringos put a lock on their basura, but the owner explained he doesn't want homeless people eating what he throws out. Pinche imbécil. You dislike him immediately.

As you approach, a sound comes from the space

behind the two dumpsters. You take three steps to the side and look. The kitchen's manager, a fat gringo named Collin who speaks horrible Spanish and sports a ridiculous mustache, is pressing Sara, one of the counter girls, against the wall. She's whimpering. He smiles at you and then tells you to fuck off, beaner.

Collin's head bounces off the wall with a loud crack. Your boot sets his jaw at a weird angle. That causes the second crack. A kick to the ribs only brings a loud exhalation. You imagine a dying buffalo and kick him again. And again. Sara screams at you. Tiene dos hijos. Su marido está preso. No tiene papeles. Este es el único trabajo que ha podido conseguir. She walks over to you and pushes you away from the piece of shit on the ground.

You drop the key on Collin and then get rid of your apron and do the same. You walk out of that filthy alley without entering the kitchen again and never go back to that place.

Julio comes around the next day and tells you to get in the car. You're going to meet a man about a job, but this is the last time he's helping you out. He sounds pissed. You don't explain yourself.

Julio tells you he talked to Silvio and your uncle told him to let you fend for yourself if you want to play hero. Eventually Julio pulls up in front of a house and tells you to knock on the door and say you still smell like the river and want to make some money. That's when you meet Guillermo. That's probably the thing that, more than anything, led to the pulsating egg in your skull. He's the man you have a message for, the man Indio kept calling "el gordo."

Now you drive as the sky starts turning orange. Every feeling in the world is inside you, but none of them stay put long enough to be identified and dealt with. You need to stop shaking. You need to pop some pills and sleep for half a day. You need to get the images of a beheading out of your skull. But you can't. You keep seeing the blood flowing out of Nestor's neck, his face scrunching up. You keep seeing Indio's arm moving the knife back and forth. You keep hearing the crack of Nestor's neck once Indio reached his spine and smacked his head to the side. You keep hearing the fucking impossible crunch coming from the bucket.

Around you, the streets seem to have taken on a new kind of darkness, one that has nothing to do with it being night or the lack of stars. You try to concentrate on driving, on moving away from what you saw and toward home and, as soon as the sun rises, a chat with Guillermo, who suddenly strikes you as the only man in the world who can help you fix this new problem you only think you understand.

You get home and walk straight to the Santa Muerte in the little table in the living room. She looks back at you with empty eye sockets that hold all the darkness in the world. You feel better. Nothing will come to get you while you're next to her. You take some pills and walk back to the statue. The sofa is closer to her than the bed, so you lie down on it and think about disappearing.

3
Laws of physics
Emotional hurricanes – UFO movies
Menudo – Pozole – Tamales
La limpia

Two objects can't occupy the same space at the same, but feelings are different. That's the important part. That's what Lauryn Hill didn't tell you. That's what I was trying to get under control that morning. I was angry and scared and felt lonely and wanted revenge and wanted to move elsewhere and wished that everything had been a nightmare and prayed to Santa Muerte for protection and missed my home, my mom, and my friends.

Two oxies are the best way to kill emotional hurricanes.

After taking the pills, I took a long shower. The oxys were working fast. The edges were turning round, and the crippling darkness in my brain started to recede.

I got out of the shower and dressed. Finally, I stepped out of the house into a glare so bright it reminded me of UFO movies and closed the door behind me.

Then I heard my name.

31

Every muscle in my body tensed. Fear and recognition jockeyed for position inside me, crushing everything else in the process.

I turned around expecting to find a guy with a gun. Instead, I found Yolanda.

The sun haloed her afro from behind. Her café con leche skin made me wish I'd known more words just so I could describe it. As always, her face was makeup-free. Ella le deja eso de la pintura a los payasos. She seemed to be allergic to sleeves. A huge sunflower blossomed on her left shoulder.

"How's it going? You okay? You look like you had a rough night."

I smiled at her. Oxy makes smiling easier.

My brain was telling me to take a few steps forward, hug her, and lose myself in her smell. A different part of me wanted to fuck her to death and then greedily suck the marrow from her bones.

"Yeah, I'm good. How you doing?"

"You sure about that? You look a little pale."

"Rough night. Don't worry about it. What are you up to today?"

She turned to the side and stuck her key in the door. Her ass was jacked up by killer high heels.

"I'm done with school for the day, so I'm just gonna take a nap and watch something on Netflix. You?"

I wanted to reply to her, but all I could think about was lying down so she could stick one of her heels into my heart and put an end to my misery. How do you tell a woman you like that you're a fucking coward? How do you explain that some bad men scared you last night and that you're on your way to see a fat bastard who you hope will take care of the problem quickly so you can sleep soundly? The answer is you don't. Everyone talks a big game about honesty, but that's a rare thing. Most people aren't honest with themselves, so they can't be honest with others. At least I'm honest with myself. I know I'm a coward. I have no problem with that. I like running away from shit and staying alive. Sue me. That was the truth, but that was not what I was about to say to a gorgeous mulata who was looking at me with her head tilted to the side and half a smile on her face that was hot enough to melt steel.

"I have to go talk to my boss. Nothing important. What are you gonna watch?"

"Problems at the club last night? My friend Juliet loves that place. Maybe you've seen her. She's about my height, purple hair…"

"A few hundred girls walk into the bar every night, and at least half of them have purple, blue, green or pink hair. Tell your friend to talk to me next time she's in there. I'll tell Martin to hook her up with some free drinks."

"Oh, yeah?"

"Yeah, and you should come with her."

"You know I don't drink."

"I'll get you some apple juice."

She looked down at her keys. I knew the conversation was over. A part of me wanted to say something, anything, to keep it going. This was not going to lead to anything, but talking to her kept me mellow and made the bad stuff recede into a dark corner of my brain.

"Alright, I'm gonna take that nap. I'll catch you later."

"Have a good one, Yoli."

She walked into her apartment and closed the door. I walked to my car and got in. Suddenly the idea of explaining everything to Guillermo scared me. The man was more likely to ignore everything than to move a finger in my defense. Still, knowing that Consuelo would be there was enough to make me stab the key into the ignition and crank my old pedazo de basura to life.

Consuelo lived with Guillermo, but they weren't related nor were they involved in any kind of standard relationship. In fact, the only thing most people knew about the arrangement was that, at some point, Consuelo had saved Guillermo's life and the two had been together ever since. Their living together was not something people really cared all that much about and there was no reason to think about it too hard. Guillermo was the boss, if you didn't count his brother, who ran everything from a shiny office in Dallas, where he pretended to be a legit businessman.

Regardless of what they were to each other, Consuelo meant the world to me. After meeting her for the first time at Guillermo's house, she asked me to come back and see her for a limpia and a talk. I had no one else in Austin, so I waited a few days and showed up early.

Consuelo gave me the limpia and then offered me coffee. I ended up telling her everything about my life back in DF, how I ended up in trouble, and that I thought of myself as a coward for running to the US when things got ugly. Somehow I ended up crying while she held me and repeated, "Tranquilo, mijo, todo va a estar bien."

After proving that I knew enough English to work wherever Guillermo decided to set me up, I had to drop by almost daily and give him a play-by-play of the previous night and hand him the money. I'm sure he did it to test me, to see if I was cutting into his cash or something. During these visits, I always ended up spending time with Consuelo. Those visits made me feel loved, welcome, cared for. Consuelo would always have a warm plate for me. Menudo. Pozole. Tamales. Pescado frito. Enchiladas rojas y verdes. Chilaquiles. Mole. Chiles en nogada con elotes frescos. Tacos al pastor. You name it, she could prepare it better than anyone.

The food was outstanding and the talks were even better. Consuelo quickly became my confidant, my guía espiritual, something like a madrecita and an abuela rolled into one. She was the first person I loved after leaving home, after feeling sad and lonely and like I would be sour and unhappy forever. She was the first person I really cared about after thinking I'd never care about anyone else ever again.

Consuelo era luz, era paz.

She was always what I needed and now I needed her more than ever.

4

Espíritus malos
Mexico es un monstruo
La luz – Warm egg – Dogs
That's Ogún

Outside my window, the city went on as if nothing had happened. People jogged, ran around on their bikes, and walked their dogs. The brutality I'd seen the previous night belonged elsewhere. It belonged in Mexico. Except Indio's eyes. Those belonged to a place that's not a place, un lugar lleno de maldad. Remembering his eyes made me feel like la huesuda was running her thin, cold fingers down my back. I asked Santa Muerte for protection once more and thought about home.

Mexico es un monstruo. It devours people. It's a dark place where bad things hide everywhere and evil people can be found around every corner. DF es una bestia gris that feeds on nine million souls every day. Los pinches gringos only care about what happens in la frontera because it's close to them, they can smell la sangre y ver los muertos, but the beating heart of Mexico is DF, and it's a black, polluted heart where bodies are found en las alcantarillas, girls are raped on buses in front of eyes that are only pretending to be blind, and people disappear without a trace way too often.

Mexico es una ciudad donde nadie es intocable.

Crazy as it sounds, I miss it. I left because someone was coming for me, and after five years away, now the same thing was happening. This time, I felt there was no place to run to. Austin was home. Don't ask me how or why, but that's how it felt.

Austin es diferente a Mexico, pero no demasiado. It has a nice face, but it's as ugly as any other big city inside. There are young people walking the streets and too many damn parks and a lot of neon lights that seem to suck the danger out of the night air, so it's easy to think nothing bad happens here. That's wrong. Downtown Austin is full of junkies and East Austin is crawling with people who have been pushed into lives of crime because the university and the government and the never-ending list of tech companies keep bringing educated hijos de puta to town and they take all the jobs. And then there are people like Guillermo, a man who lives off the city's vices como una remora gorda con bigote. This is a nice city the way New York is a nice city, which is to say that it only looks perfect if you don't look too hard.

The drive to Guillermo's house was quick. He lived on a short street near MoPac, the dividing line between los Mexicanos y negros del norte and the rich white folks of Westlake Hills.

I parked in front of his house and walked up to the door. Instead of knocking, which usually gets Consuelo's pack of dogs howling, I sent Guillermo a text. He replied almost immediately, saying the door was open.

The house was a three-room, one-bathroom joint with a dirty beige carpet covering the living room floor. There was a huge brown L-shaped sofa a few feet from the door. In front of it sat a TV that was a few inches short of a movie theater screen. I'd never seen it turned on. Instead, Guillermo always hung out in the second room on the right.

As expected, I could see Consuelo in the kitchen, wearing one of her usual batas de noche, this one deep blue and full of red flowers. She smiled as I came in. I looked at her, smiled back. Sus cejas came together like two rams head-butting each other.

"Ay, mijo, estás rodeado de oscuridad!"

"Lo sé, tuve una mala noche."

I kept my reply as cool as possible, but I knew she could read my soul. She could see the thing following me around like one of those black clouds en los muñequitos.

"Come, Fernando, come," she said, waving me over.

I walked to the kitchen. Consuelo was waiting for me with her arms open, her six dogs standing next to her legs. I walked into her hug, bending over a little, and placed my head on her shoulder. She smelled of great food and that particular abuela smell that penetrates right down to your soul and makes you feel like a kid. Consuelo caressed my head and for a second I felt like I could take a nap right there, that no one could ever harm me in any way and that all bad thoughts would leave me, pushed away by the softness and warmth of her arms. Then she let me go, stepped back, caught her breath, and pulled out a chair for me. She signaled for me to sit and moved toward the fridge. The dogs followed her like they were tied to her short legs with a very short leash.

Consuelo closed the fridge's door and turned around. She had an egg in her right hand.

"You don't have to tell me what happened to you, but at least let me give you a limpia, mijito. It'll help. Te lo aseguro."

"You know Nestor?"

"¿El muchacho que trabajaba contigo?"

"Ese mismo."

"What happened to him? Did he do something to you?"

"No, Nestor won't be doing much of anything any more. Lo mataron anoche. Yo estaba allí cuando paso."

"¿Quién lo mató?"

"I don't know. Unos pinches mareros. De la Salvatrucha. Bad guys. They had a message for Guillermo. That's why I'm here."

"Watching someone die is a bad thing, Fernando, su fantasma se puede pegar a ti, pedir que lo vengues. Eso es una responsabilidad muy, muy grande. But a simple ghost doesn't explain what I see around you. This thing you're dragging around is heavier. It's sharp. Peligrosa. I don't like it. Tienes que sacarte de emcima lo que sea que agarraste anoche, mijo. No se puede andar así por la vida."

One of Consuelo's dogs let out a yelp that seemed to echo the old woman's feelings. I looked down at the chingo. It looked back at me with eyes that spoke of more intelligence than those of half the people I had to talk to every night.

"El hombre que lo hizo, un tal Indio…he had black eyes. Y muchos tatuajes que…I don't know, I think I saw them move. He also made a weird prayer as he killed Nestor, something about Ogún. No era español. It was something else. It made me feel cold. I was scared, Consuelo. I still am."

Consuelo looked at me. Telling her I was scared was my way of asking her for protection. She was the kind of woman you can't lie to because she can see through you, her eyes never getting stuck on the veil. She came toward me. Her dogs followed. The one she'd had the longest, a black and brown mutt she called Kahlúa, looked at me and whimpered. I looked at her and, for the millionth time, thought that dog had human eyes and a brain to match. Consuelo's dogs weren't violent, but they scared me because they seemed to understand everything that went on around them. They seemed to communicate with Consuelo without language and acted as if they understood every word that came out of anyone's mouth.

Consuelo placed her hand on my shoulder and I took my eyes off the chingos.

"Ogún is the god of iron and war. He is a very violent god. The man who killed Nestor was probably praying to him, offering Nestor's blood as sacrifice. Elegguá opens the roads, but it is Ogún that clears the roads with his powerful machete. Los hijos de Ogún wear green and black necklaces and they pray to him whenever they take a life. Ogún oko dara obaniché aguanile ichegún iré. The prayer is to make sure that Ogún accepts the sacrifice, that the spilling of blood pleases him. It helps the killer keep los espíritus vengativos away. The prayer is a way of not having to deal with the anger and bad energy caused by a murder. Las vibraciones que dejan los muertos son una cosa muy, muy poderosa, Fernando. Ogún himself isn't too bad when those praying to him are gente Buena, gente que tiene el alma pura. He's the protector of metal workers. However, he's also the god violent soldiers pray to, and it sounds like this man is one of those, mijo, un asesino."

"Nando, get your ass in here!"

Guillermo's voice put an end to Consuelo's words. She looked toward the hallway and shook her head.

"Go and see him ahora, mijito. Tell him what's going on. These men are crazy. Guillermo has dealt with planty of crazy men before and he will know what to do now. When you're done with him, come back here so I can give you that limpia and a novena para que reces estos días. De verdad necesitas ambas cosas."

I nodded and got up.

Guillermo was sitting on a brown recliner. A small TV sat atop a black coffee table in front of him. Two black ladies were screaming at each other onscreen. They waved their hands around, each full of nails so long they could probably scratch the back of their skulls every time they dug for a moco. Their screams mixed with the music coming from a boom box on the floor next to Guillermo's chair. Algo con mucho acordeón y una voz chillona. As always, that combination took me back to that long ride in a stinky van with a quiet coyote. Why Guillermo had a TV and a radio always going at once was something I never understood. In the right corner of the room, below the room's only window, was a second chair with an old blue guayabera draped over it. The shirt, according to Guillermo, had once belonged to Niño Fidencio. He'd paid $200 en un Mercado de pulgas for it. Underneath the chair, a candle with Niño Fidencio's face on it burned. Guillermo didn't leave his house much, but he somehow managed to always have a supply of candles at hand. Next to the chair was a stuffed gallo de pelea. His feathers were puffed out and his beak was open. It looked like it could give the bravest kid in the neighborhood the worst pesadillas he ever had.

"Hola, mi amigo."

Guillermo's voice made me think of a frog. He looked like he had fallen back into the chair. His prodigious gut was pushing against his yellow shirt and his blue shorts would only look good in man a third his size. His face was relaxed, his pupils dilated to the size of dimes. He smiled at me slowly, the way people do when they're looking at you and suddenly remember something stupid you said or did. I didn't have to ask to know he had just fixed himself, but that slo-mo smile gave it away. Maybe this wasn't the best time to talk to him about the previous night.

"How's it going, Guillermo?" I replied in English because saying *Hola, mi amigo* and ordering tacos was all he could say in Spanish. Los padres de Guillermo tenían miedo de que su hijo fuera discriminado, así que nunca le enseñaron español. Pendejos.

"I don't know, Nando. You tell me. I wasn't expecting you until Friday or maybe Saturday morning. Now you're here and Consuelo sounds concerned. If you don't have some money for me and drop by to talk, it's usually because you need me to help you with something."

He was right, but I didn't feel bad about that. He was my boss. He made sure the drugs reached my hands and I made sure the money reached his. No teníamos por qué ser cuates. I had asked for some help at the beginning with things like getting my hands on a fake license and buying a car with fake papers and insurance. Though I hadn't asked him for help with anything like that in years, he liked to remind me how many favors he had done for me. I worked hard for him and never cheated him out of a fucking centavo, so I figured we were a mano.

Guillermo closed his eyes and dropped his massive jowls onto his chest. The caballo was riding his veins hard because it was still fresh. If I talked for too long, the chances of him slipping away to a better place increased. Tenía que decirle algo que fuera como un golpe, something that would hit him as hard as the perla negra filling his body with warmth and his head with gentle nothingness.

"They killed Nestor last night. I was there when it happened. A motherfucker had him tied to a chair. He chopped his head off with a knife."

Guillermo sat up. His eyes turned into black slits. For a second I expected him to laugh, to say I was pulling his leg. Instead, he slowly brought a hand up and touched his moustache, which wouldn't be out of place on a walrus.

"Take a seat and tell me what happened."

He signaled to the chair across from him. I sat down, suddenly realizing the air in the room was heavy with old sweat and fat man farts.

I told him the story until I had to stop. The images were coming back and taking my breath away. I wanted to cry. I wanted to run back and ask Consuelo to make all the bad memories go away with some of her magic.

"You okay?"

Guillermo's question was stupid. I wasn't okay and wouldn't be okay for a long time. Going on was my only choice, and I was starting to question my commitment to it.

"A man named Indio wanted me to give you a message."

"A message?"

"He said they want to run things downtown between I-35 and Mopac and from MLK all the way down to the river. He said you can keep the rest and…"

"Wait, wait, wait," said Guillermo. I didn't know if his doped brain was processing everything too slow or if he was unclear on the facts. "So you're telling me this motherfucker killed Nestor to scare your ass into submission and then basically said he wants the heart of Austin for himself?"

"He also said you don't have to give everything away, just work with them," I said.

"Fucking fantastic! So I get to work just as hard as I work now but, instead of keeping my money, I can give it away to some fucking gangbanging monkeys with tattooed faces? You understand what you're saying to me right now, Fernando? Did this son of a bitch at least tell you if he was working for a cartel? Did he mention the Sinaloa Cartel sending him? Did he say he was delivering a message from the Gulf Cartel? Anything other than the MS-13?"

More than angry, Guillermo seemed surprised and a bit amused, as if what I was saying were nothing more than the most ridiculous joke he had ever heard. Maybe the barro Mexicano running through his veins had something to do with that.

"No, Guillermo. They just said they were from la Salvatrucha and that they came to town to take over. They killed Nestor and told me they wouldn't mind getting their hands even dirtier if you didn't agree to their terms."

"Listen, Nando, I like you. You work hard and don't run around flashing your cash and drawing attention to yourself. You show up on time and don't let those pills you take interfere with your work. We've never had any problems and you always deliver your money untouched. But this is fucking ridiculous. I can't just pick up the phone and tell my brother to send some reinforcements because some gangbangers scared the shit out of you last night. Austin belongs to the Zetas and you know that. Everyone knows that. If these guys that picked you and Nestor up last night don't know that, they're bound to find out soon enough. They'd be crazy to mess with us if they knew, and once they know, they'll disappear and move to California or something. The Salvatrucha packs a mighty punch south of the border, but here, they're nothing. They're idiots who apparently don't mind getting killed for a few bucks and nothing more. That's why La Eme sends them on suicide missions; they're fools who like violence but never cover their asses. I've never had to worry about them and I don't really think I should start doing it now."

Guillermo stopped and looked at me in silence for a few seconds. Every time he blinked, it looked like he had to fight to lift his párpados again.

"I know los Zetas are in control here and I know no mareros should be crazy enough to come fuck with us, but they did. Indio is not like other mareros I've met, man. It's like he enjoys being evil. He was smiling while he cut Nestor's head off. He's crazy enough to kill me and then come after you. I wouldn't lie to you, Guillermo. You know I wouldn't. This is not about a couple of newbie gangbangers talking big game. These dudes had all kinds of ink on them. They've all done hard time."

"Do you really think these motherfuckers are gonna cause trouble again?"

I wanted to tell Guillermo about Indio's eyes. I wanted to make him understand that there was something at the bottom of that bucket and that it ate Nestor's severed fingers. However, every combination of words, every explanation my brain came up with sounded loco.

"Listen, Guillermo, they fucking chopped Nestor's head off ..."

"Okay," he interrupted, "You think it's serious. I'm gonna give Neal a call and tell him to go looking for some dudes with tattooed faces running around town. They're probably new, so they have to be out and about, getting booze, drugs, and pussy somewhere in town. Neal will talk to them."

Neal was a mountain of a man who used to play football for UT. A teammate found some gay pornography in his car and started cracking jokes. Neal beat him all the way to death's door, raped him, and left him there, spitting teeth and shitting blood. He was kicked out of the university and never played football again. He didn't serve time because the guy he left for dead refused to press charges. Neal had been working as hired muscle ever since. Usually he didn't even have to hit people because of his size, which is why many businesses used him as a collector. However, he was not the man for this job. The size of Neal's arms wouldn't really matter to the kind of men who had kidnapped me.

"You send Neal their way and, if he can find them, you'll be responsible for Neal's death. And they're probably going to be pissed that you tried to scare them off with a fucking gorilla and then come looking for you."

Guillermo was not the kind of guy who took it lightly when someone disagreed with him, so I expected him to start screaming. Instead he sighed, rubbed his left arm, and looked at the guayabera on the chair. He spoke again, his voice calmer than I expected.

"So you want me to call my brother and tell him to send El Príncipe? That crazy motherfucker will flaunt his guns around and scare everyone in sight if he doesn't shoot himself in the dick first."

El Príncipe was a guy Raúl, Guillermo's brother, had on his team and brought along whenever he traveled. He was born in Puerto Rico to a wealthy family and started selling drugs because a friend told

50

him having street cred was the only way to get his career as a reggaetón singer off the ground. He was in a few mixtapes and sang a big game, always rapping about selling kilos, making tons of paper, shooting people, and getting pussy. Then another singer, a man who went by Killa or some shit like that, was released from prison. Killa had done a few years on a weapons possession charge that fell on top of the drug charges that were already hanging over him. Soon after he was released, he dropped a tiraera song calling El Príncipe a rich kid with less street cred than Ja Rule. The song didn't sit well with El Príncipe, so he went looking for the guy and popped him two times en la cara. Then he left Puerto Rico for Florida and somehow ended up becoming a hired gun instead of an artist. How he went from gangbanging in Florida to killing people for money in Dallas is a mystery to me.

"No," I said. "El Príncipe es my ruidoso. He's too obvious, too damn loud. He doesn't know how to handle really dangerous people. He thinks every situation is one of his songs. That guy belongs inside a video game, not on the streets."

"So what do you want me to do, put together an army and go after them? To kick every bush and storm into every shitty house on the east side until we find some guys with MS inked on their mugs? We can't have that kind of noise in this town, man. This isn't New Orleans or Detroit. We don't do things that way here, Nando, and you know that," said Guillermo, his face twisted like he'd just smelled putrid meat.

"No, don't put together an army, just give The Russian a call and tell him to look for four mareros covered in black ink who are living or working out of the east side and drive a huge blue car with ridiculous rims."

"The Russian? Are you kidding me? You think these gangbangers are that much of a threat?"

The Russian was an average looking middle-aged man with a thick accent who told folks he worked with plants for a living. In reality, he was a shadow made of razors, a fantasma who no one saw coming until it was too late. Anyone who had ever worked with him was satisfied, and no one dared speak ill of him because he seemed to have eyes and ears all over. If you wanted someone to disappear forever without a trace, you called The Russian. He was worth every damn penny. And he worked really cheap.

"Don't think for a second you'll be wasting money on this by calling him, Guillermo. I'm telling you these guys are for real. You weren't there. I was."

I stopped talking because I realized something was going to come out of my mouth that I didn't even know was in my head: that if he refused to call someone like The Russian, the only option I'd be left with would be to pack up all my stuff and disappear forever, just like last time.

"I'll tell you what, Nando, I'm gonna trust you on this. If you say these guys are the real deal and have bad intentions, I'll give you ten long ones to call the Russian. That's a lot of money, but if this is serious, then I guess it's worth it. When you call him, tell him to pick up the dough with Sandra, like last time. And you make it happen. Leave me out of it. Just let me know when it's done. I don't want this to come back and bite me in the ass. And I'll call my brother, ask him a few questions. Maybe he knows something or knows someone who has heard of these guys. If this is some trick or these guys are fucking nobodies with no history and no connections, I'll make you pay me back the ten thousand. You better pray you're right."

"Gracias, Guillermo."

"Call him today. I don't want this shit to interfere with your work. Are you going to the club tonight?"

"Yeah, I'll be there."

"Did they really stuff you in a trunk?"

"Yeah, they hit me with something and threw me in the trunk."

I instinctively raised my hand and gently touched the bump in the back of my skull.

"Your head okay?"

"Yeah. Nestor's isn't."

"Good. Nothing we can do about Nestor now. Let the Russian handle it. Let me know when this has been taken care of."

"You got it, Guillermo."

"Was Consuelo cooking something when you came in?"

The question threw me off. I had to think for a second. I hadn't smelled anything, and if Consuelo was cooking, you could smell her magic before you entered the house.

"No, I don't think so."

"Okay. Call me."

Guillermo looked at the TV again. The two black ladies were gone. Two talking heads in blue suits were discussing something with creepy smiles on their faces.

Probably something about building una pared en la frontera. I stood up, mumbled a goodbye mixed with a thanks and walked out of the room, craving some tamales for the second time that day.

Consuelo was waiting for me in the kitchen. She still had the egg in her hand.

"Siéntate, mijo, esto es rápido."

I walked into the kitchen and sat down. Kahlúa was looking at me with her human eyes. Something in them spoke of calm and comfort, but there was also worry in there. And fear. I almost jumped when Consuelo's hand brushed against my head.

She was saying a prayer under her breath while she rubbed my head, chest, back, shoulders with the egg. Kahlúa came over, placed her head on my right thigh, and whimpered. A second later, two more heads plopped down on my left thigh. It felt good.

After a few minutes, Consuelo stopped. She had looked well when I came in, but now she looked like she hadn't slept in three days. She grabbed my hand and placed the egg in it.

"Take this outside with you and throw it away. Don't do it in front of the house and don't get any of it on you. Piensa en las cosas malas que viste cuando lo tires. This won't take care of everything, but at least you will walk out of here with less weight on your shoulders. Ah, y reza esta novena. Get nine white candles for la Santa Muerte y pónselas a sus pies. Te va a ayudar. La Niña Blanca no defrauda a nadie."

She gave me a few pieces of paper torn from a notebook. Her handwriting was easily legible. I'd have to do the prayers for nine consecutive days, and there was a lot written. The thought crossed my mind that it was impossible for her to write so much down in the time it took me to tell Guillermo everything.

I stood up, folded the sheets, and stuffed them in my pocket.

"Gracias, Consuelo."

"De nada, mijo. Ven a verme pronto."

The way she asked me to come back and see her soon was odd, full of an urgency I'd never perceived before. I smiled at her, feeling a bit better after la limpia, and looked at the dogs crowded around her legs.

"Te quieren mucho esos chingos, Consuelo."

"Y yo a ellos, mijo, son almas viejas pagando sus penas a cuatro patas. A lot of us have to go through that process in our transition. I'm just happy to be able to help them."

I had no idea what she meant by that, but I was afraid to ask because the look on her face spoke of a deep pain. I gave her a quick hug, turned around, and left.

Once outside the house, I looked at the egg in my hand. It hadn't been out of the fridge for that long, but it felt warm, as if it'd just been pulled out of the microwave. I walked down the sidewalk for a bit because I didn't want to leave that mess in front of Guillermo's house and Consuelo had been clear about getting rid of it elsewhere.

Three or four houses later, I stopped, brought my hand up, and dropped the egg. It cracked on the sidewalk and a thick black fluid that looked like overused oil oozed out. The sun hit the inky mess and something appeared to move within it. I bent over to get a better look and saw a few thin worms squirming around in the blackness. A shiver ran down my back. It was time to go home and start my prayers.

5
White candles
Manto sagrado – The Russian
Ved'ma Nursery - Tatuirovannyye litsa
Pinche culero

One of the reasons I managed to adapt so quickly to life in Austin is that, while there are a lot of blancos moving around, you don't have to scratch the surface too hard for the city's Mexican blood to flow. Menudo, chicharrón, tequila, and totopos are as easily available here as they are on the other side of la frontera, and then there are radio stations that play nothing but música norteña, tiendas that only sell Mexican products, iglesias that offer mass in Spanish every day of the week, and many other things that make it feel like a home away from home. Another benefit of having our cultura so clavada here is that you can find candles everywhere, including the grocery store.

With the nine velas blancas set up in front of la Santa Muerte, I pulled the papers Consuelo had given me out of my pocket. I wanted to call the Russian and get everything squared with him right away, but something was telling me that praying before calling him was a good idea. I lit one of the velas and read, noticing Consuelo had left a blank space in the prayers where I was supposed to ask for my favors.

Novena a la Santa Muerte
Día 1

Santísima Muerte los favores que me tienes que conceder lograrán que venza todas las dificultades, que derrote a todos mis enemigos, y que para mi nada resulte imposible. No encontraré obstáculos insalvables en mi camino ni me toparé con enemigos que me dañen. Todos serán mis amigos y yo seré el vencedor en todas las empresas y asuntos que realice. Mi casa se llenará de bonanza con tu protección y virtudes.

Santísima Muerte, te hago esta novena para pedirte el favor de que me protejas de Indio y los hombres que trabajan para el y que sus balas y malas intenciones no me encuentren a mi antes de que tu afilada guadaña los encuentre a ellos y los elimine de mi camino. Por favor espero me concedas esta petición si es de tu placer. Que así sea.

¡Oh, *Muerte Sagrada, Reliquia de Dios, sácame de penas y peligros! Que tu ansia infinita por hacer el bien sea siempre conmigo. Desde tu esfera celeste nos cobije siempre tu Manto Sagrado, Santísima Muerte.*

I was supposed to pray three Padre Nuestros on top of that, but I decided to skip them. No need to talk to that guy when I had mi querida Niña Blanca protecting my back. The vela would eventually burn out, but hopefully not too long before I could come back and pray the second day's prayer.

I sat on the sofa and pulled my phone out of my pocket and dialed the Russian.

It only rang twice.

"Ved'ma Nursery, how may I help you?"

"Hey, man, it's Fernando," I said, suddenly short of breath and far more nervous than I thought I'd be.

"Nando, it is good to hear from you."

The Russian pronounced it "jir," just like a Mexican would, which always struck me as funny.

"It's good to talk to you, man. How are you doing?"

"Life is okay, Nando. We are all tied to it and it drags us along. Mine is not going too fast at the moment, so there is no pain. How can I help you, drug?"

This was it, the moment of truth.

"There are some men who want to hurt me and Guillermo. They want to take over the city and kick the Zetas out. They killed someone I knew, a good guy who had kids and a wife at home. I…I want them gone."

"This is no problem, this is something we can make happen. Who are these idioty and where can they be found?"

"I only know the name of one, Indio. There are probably four or five of them. They're mareros, gangbangers, and their bodies and faces are covered with tattoos. The night I met them they were driving a big, old blue car with huge shiny rims. I'm pretty sure they're spending time on the east side."

"Tatuirovannyye litsa? A lot of tattoos?" he asked.

"Yeah, a lot. The one they call Indio basically has a black face by now. He's easy to spot."

"This is a good thing. This will make finding them easy. Guillermo say anything about money to you or are you paying me?"

"Yeah, Guillermo said you can pick up the dough with Sandra."

"If you pay, I give you discount, but if Guillermo pay, I will accept it all. That zhir ublyudok is too lazy for a discount, he has to pay full price. And you should have brought me the money to some place. Last time, it was nice talking to you. I enjoyed learning about your saint and your trip across the border. This city is full of people from other places. This is something I like. It makes us invisible."

The Russian chuckled and then coughed. Payment had been discussed and I'd given him everything I had on the mareros. Now I only had to wait until this nightmare was officially over.

"Thanks. Please let me know when…you've taken care of things."

"This I will do."

The Russian hung up. He didn't ask for my number or tell me how long he thought it would take. However, having someone like him gunning for Indio made me feel better. Ese pinche culero no le iva a cortar la cabeza a nadie más. Soon those tattooed monkeys would be nothing more than a bad memory. The Russian was going to make them disappear forever. The death of someone else had never made me feel so good.

I texted Guillermo saying I made the call and then stuck the phone back in my pocket. Then I sat there in silence, staring at the deep darkness in Santa Muerte's eyes. For those of us who were on her good side, that darkness was welcoming, like a place to hide in a violent storm. For those who were on her bad side, that darkness was a promise of death that brought destruction of the soul as well as of the flesh. The thought almost made me smile.

6
La frontera redux
The blood of innocents – La migra
Pinche gringo pendejo
Skeletons

What happens when you cross la frontera is that you leave a place to enter a void. You vacate a known reality and change it for something that you have to force yourself to believe, to accept, to understand.

What happens when you cross la frontera is that you shed un pedazo grande of your identity and become a different thing, something that's part apparition, part useless flesh, and part broken memories. You abandon familia, amigos, lenguaje, and the streets you know for a place where you have no rights and are not even considered a citizen, a country in which you will live like a stowaway rat, always afraid of being discovered. So you change. You morph. Te vuelves otra cosa. You start speaking English fast in hopes that your brown skin will be ignored if you at least communicate well. You dress yourself with the comics you read and the books you hated in school and the movies you've watched since you were a kid and that thing becomes el nuevo tu. You cover your tatuajes and learn that people on the streets will remember you only if you speak Spanish in their presence. You do everything in your power to become a gringo, to fit in, to become as unnoticeable as the cracks in the sidewalks. Then you start walking with less confidence because everything is mysterious and new and scary and you never feel bienvenido.

What happens when you cross la frontera is that la frontera keeps a piece of you, cuts you inside, hasta el hueso, where you can't heal yourself. It slashes you in places no blade or bullet can reach and cripples you in ways you don't understand.

Cruzar la frontera fucks you over en formas que no sabías que podías ser jodido.

What happens when you cross la frontera is that your body becomes a magnet for the bad stuff that has piled up all along that awful dividing line.

Muerte.

Destrucción.

Desesperación.

Olvido.

La nada infinita.

La noche eterna full of screams.

Crossing la frontera is like crossing a swamp because you end up covered in unpleasant shit no matter what you do. La frontera is a place of crying espíritus. It's a place of almas perdidas y en pena, all of them looking for a way back, for a way to undo what happened, for a path back to their loved ones and their known places and a time before they made their awful decision.

La frontera is a place where miedo seeps into your bones and the silence you're forced to keep allows the cries of dead children to enter your soul and break you in half like a dry twig. La frontera is a place where los huesos de los muertos are never buried deep enough and the pain of broken familias and la sangre de los inocentes has mixed with the plants and the air and the soil. All that darkness is what gives el río its peculiar smell and green color. Some things have a bottom but they are bottomless. The infinite darkness that hides in that flowing jade vein is what makes white men with guns pull the trigger even when the figure moving under the crosshairs is a woman or a child.

What happens when you cross la frontera is that you shatter, you stop being you and turn into a new person that belongs nowhere, that has no home, no roots. Going back is impossible and moving forward is like jumping into a ravine and hoping that it's not too deep, that the rocks don't mangle you too much, and that el monstruo that waits for you en la oscuridad is not too hungry.

What happens when you cross la frontera is that you have to do whatever it takes to survive, and that's what pushes you into a life of crime. You need money to survive and washing dishes or mowing lawns are easy gigs to get but they don't pay enough. In this country, fairness is a concept and nothing more. Los pinches gringos will send dinero to Africa and will pay thousands of dollars to chop their cat's huevos off and remove their nails, but they won't pay you a fair amount for painting their fucking mansiones and, if you complain, te llaman a la migra. Pinches hijueputas. Why the fuck should you do stuff in this country that you would never have done back home? Why should you smell like the shit you have to clean when you used to roll around with chingos de lana in your pocket? Thinking about that either makes you look for something different or breaks you again.

What happens when you cross la frontera is that you want to clean up, find a good job somewhere, meet a beautiful, sweet girl. You want the American Dream. But fuck all that. The American Dream is as false as the meat in your one-dollar burger and the canned laughter you hear on television. And it's even worse for you. You have no skills and no diploma and no friends and no nada. You're a problem. Un ilegal más. A beaner. A television joke. A wetback. You're nothing but an issue brainless white politicians discuss from the safety of their offices. That's when any offer becomes salvation, any desperate move a solution, every bad idea something that gives you a bit of hope. That's when you realize that you will always live in a silent war and that anyone who's not from your patria can be your enemy at any moment. That's why you easily fall into selling rich white kids drugs while you pretend to work security at a bar.

Desperation leads to the gig at the door and the gig at the door leads to some money and the bills in your pocket leads to a sense of accomplishment. You talk to Guillermo and he talks to a white college student who drives a shiny new BMW and asks you for $400 cash and leases a one-bedroom apartment under his name and hands you the key. "You pull any stunts, I'll have my friends find you. You don't want that to happen, amigo," he says. You smile, nod. Pinche gringo pendejo playing tough guy. You want to tell him *No mames, güey* while you grab him by the throat and slam his head against the pavement until his brain comes out his nose. You want to fill his stupid mouth with dirt so he can feel what many others feel as they try to cross la frontera and end up with their faces in the dirt as the sun devours the flesh of their backs. But you don't. You stay put and put all your strength on ignoring your desires. Instead of teaching the huevón a lesson, you take the keys he's holding out to you and enter your new casa for the first time ever. Then you put a mattress on the floor and a small television next to it. You put some food in the fridge and build your altar and start trying to convince yourself that it isn't so bad. Then you settle in somewhat and stay away from the leasing office, never check your mail, and get the fuck out of there for the entire day whenever they leave a note on the door saying someone will be entering the apartment to kill some cucarachas or check the batteries en los detectores de humo. You don't know it yet, but this vida de mentira, this hiding around, it starts turning you into a ghost, a transparency on two legs, a shadow that's not attached to anything solid. Then, when you notice, you also realize that being almost invisible is helpful and that your indistinctness is the only reason no one really notices you working the door at the bar and selling all sorts of overpriced pharmaceuticals to kids who think they're really cool.

You're in the corazón of a large city, completely exposed for hours to thousands of faces that come to 6th Street to drink and dance and try to fuck someone, but no one pays attention to you. You're a darker spot moving within a charco de sombra, just another brown face in a town where brown faces look out at you from every drive thru window and brown hands clean every car and a woman from a country south of the border cleans every mansion and every landscaping crew is full of guys who look just like you and every precious toddler at the park knows a bit of Spanish because his nanny only speaks Spanish when mommy and daddy aren't around.

What happens when you cross la frontera is that you don't know what's going to happen to you and you hustle harder than you ever hustled before and you pray to la Santa Muerte and ask for protección and do bad things that you convince yourself are not that bad because la frontera crossed your abuelos first and no one is really pinche ilegal because people can't be ilegal and we're all atrapados en este puto mundo. Then you try to forget about everything that came before, you try to pretend like the familia and the women and the amigos and the laughter and the fear and the bodies and the money and the years are just not there and you focus on making money, staying alive, and being invisible. And the easiest way to be invisible is to be in front of a lot of eyes that don't give a shit.

Working at the club is the best way to make money and hide in plain sight. Most Mexicans come to this country and end up doing backbreaking work for fucking centavos because they're afraid of la migra and think being out in the open and having a visible job will lead to deportation. Al carajo eso. You do what you have to do and even learn to enjoy it a little because you can pay your bills and have plenty of pills at home and own a car and a gun and an iPod full of buena música and even have more than enough lana at home to replace the iPod some pinches mareros stole from you.

What sometimes happens when you cross la frontera is that you go to work the night after some assholes kidnapped you and chopped someone's head off right in front of you. Being there is weird and your butt clenches every time you think about walking to your car alone after all the rich white drunks have gone back to their homes and dorms, but it also makes you feel like life is already doing its thing and moving on. Because the thing about life is that time gets between facts and memories and as memories turn into what they are, facts start sliding back, moving into a space full of images from películas and skeletons from bad dreams and imagined monstruos and stuff that someone told you. That makes the fear lessen. Then you start thinking about the Russian cruising around in a car like a hungry predator looking for prey. You think about his gun spitting out justice and someone's head hitting the pavement with a loud thud and blood running down into the gutter. Between that thought and the knowledge that la Santísima Muerte is watching your back, you give folks their drugs, stuff the money they hand over into your pocket before transferring it to the little box behind the bar, pop a few oxies, and walk to your car without looking back every two seconds while you wish for the call that will let you know que la muerte ha hecho su trabajo.

7
The End of Days
Heroin – weed – blow
The last working horse of the Blues
Never let them see you scared

Yeah, that night I went to work. I was scared. I had no gun. I wanted to stay home, locked away and safe, but that's not the way to do things. You can't let them see you scared. Bad people are like dogs. They can smell your fear. That's when they pounce on you y te obligan a repartir chingazos o morir como una rata.

I stood at my spot at the door of The Jackalope and actually wished a few caras palidas with popped collars would start some shit just so I could throw them out.

A white kid wearing a ball cap and sunglasses came up to me and asked me for for a quarter in a nervous voice. I had some Blue Dream, a few dime bags of White Rhino, and a few old bags of a shitty shipment of Death Star that apparently was as strong as oregano. Only idiots wear sunglasses and caps at night, so I told the kid forty for two quarters and handed him the Death Star. No tenia ni idea de lo que estaba comprando.

Folks came in and out like any other night, but I was paying special attaention to every face. I was on the lookout for inked features.

My second client of the night was a regular. Horse was a black man who played the blues at The Rollins Bar. He came over, gave me a quick hug/handshake and got his stuff. Then, like always, he leaned against the wall next to me and started talking about everything and nothing all at once.

"Man, they have some rigid mufuckas in there tonight," he said, pointing down the sidewalk at The Rollins Bar. "Why the fuck you gonna go to a blues bar if you're more worried about talking on your phone than listening to some tunes? People stupid. People always been stupid, but this shit is getting ridiculous. Don't know how much longer I'm gonna be able to do my thing, man, you know what I mean? I'm old, man. You can't keep the last working horse of the blues going in these mufucking conditions. I done played with Lightnin' Hopkins back in the day. I played harp with SRV for a few gigs before he hit it big, man. These ain't no conditions for a living legend, you know what I mean? Fucking playing for rigid ass mufuckas."

Horse shook his head, thanked me, and left. I'm no blues historian, but he regularly told stories of playing with blues legends in San Antonio back in the 30s and 40s. O es un vampiro negro o un hijueputa mentiroso.

About an hour after Horse disappeared back into the night, I spotted Pilar making her way down 6th Street toward me. No one knew her last name, age or country of origin. All we knew about her was that she did a lot of heroin and constantly spoke about the final judgement in a bizarre, diluted accent that could be from Puerto Rico, Cuba or the Dominican Republic. Rumors, por otro lado, were abundant. Some said she had a PhD in something and worked as a professor for many years before losing a baby and turning to smack for comfort. Others said she was a ghost trapped on 6ᵗʰ Street, un espíritu con algún propósito aún por cumplir.

A block away, her words were reaching my ears above the usual escándalo of the street.

"The Almighty is giving you a chance to stop sinning right now," she was saying. "I am His voice, here to warn you of the coming judgement. You who obey the needs of the flesh now will soon be cast into the flaming pits of eternal damnation!"

Someone yelled at her to shut up from inside a bar. It stopped her in her tracks. She looked around, her eyes wide and her hands out wide.

"Have fun now, you son of a whore, for you will be the first to cry when the seas blacken, the mountains turn to dust, and the Almighty starts striking down the sinners! You will see your mother eating your father and everything you love will be covered first in hungry locusts and then in the darkness and stench of decay!"

She finally reached me and came in for the transaction. I had her bag of peace ready to go because her smell was hard to put up with, so I always tried to get her taken care of and back on her way as quickly as possible. This time, however, she stopped a few feet away. I look at her wild hair and ojos locos and went back to paying attention to the door. You can't worry too much about the things junkies do.

"Your time is closer than theirs," said Pilar. I looked back at her. Her eyes were locked into mine, wide open and bloodshot.

"You will be gone before the streets of this town are covered in the bodies of men and beasts. The Fallen Angel is reaching out for you, his filthy talons craving the feel of your ripping flesh."

Her words sent a shiver down my spine.

"Get away from my door, Pilar. I can't have you here spitting nonsense at the customers."

"Repent now. Your time is almost at hand. When you start coughing up blood and hear the hoofs of the Beast on your roof, remember my wor…"

"Get out of here, Pilar. I don't want to have to remove you."

She looked at me. She turned around and walked down the sidewalk in silence.

Pilar's words wouldn't have worried me, but the fact that she left without her smack and cut out her crazy talk made me feel very uncomfortable. The feeling grew inside me and morphed into something cold that stuck to my ribs.

After the doors closed, I pretended to be feeling very tired and asked Jenny, a waitress whose boyfriend always picked her up at the end of the night, to give me a ride to my car.

8
Too much zlo
Tchort – Men with black eyes
Dueña Poderosa de la Negra Mansión
Belly full of razorblades

The Russian called me the next morning. My head spun from too many pills and I was nauseous, but the pills had helped me sleep. I picked up the phone and looked at it. As always, the number on the screen was not the same number I'd called, and I knew it was a number I'd never see again. I swiped my finger across the screen and placed the phone against my ear with a smile plastered on my sleepy face. The chemical cocktail cruising through my system made the sheets feel like feathers brushing against my skin.

"Hello?"

"I found the men you wanted me to find," the Russian said, sounding tired. I imagined Nestor's soul flying into the body of a fly just so he could land on Indio's glassy eye and take a shit on it. Thinking about him made me sad, but the idea that a threat that had been hovering over me like a jealous helicopter was now gone trumped that sadness.

"I knew you would. You always get things done. That's why I called you. So…everything has been taken care of? Easy job?"

"No, Nando. I am sorry. This is not something I can help you with. This is something I don't think anyone can help you with. Too much…zlo involved."

I didn't know what *zlo* meant but, for a second, I didn't really care because I thought he was joking, so I stayed quiet. I expected him to laugh and then tell me everything was fine. He didn't. The threat was back, now more menacing than ever. If Indio and his monkeys had evaded The Russian or, even worse, spotted him and figured out why he was there and who had sent him, I would be in even deeper trouble.

"What are you talking about?"

"These men, Nando, they are all working for a man who has black eyes. They are full of very plokhoy chernila. My father, he told to me stories of a man like that when I was growing up, a man who lived alone in the woods with a dog and never aged. He would come out of the taiga once in a while and go to town to buy vodka and bread, never something more. No one looked this man in the eyes because they sometimes looked black when he returned the stare. When someone went missing who didn't have any trouble with anyone, people always said that the black-eyed man took them, that he ate their heart and trapped their dusha. They said that kept him young, the blood, the killing. My father said the man had made a deal with Tchort and was no longer human, that he was a monster that belonged to hell. I never believed him, but a few years after my father's death I came across this man while walking with my mother. He looked at her and winked. Then he stuck his tongue out, and incredibly long tongue, and moved it like at snake at my mother. She saw him, closed her eyes, and touched the rosary around her neck. She stood still and prayed with her eyes closed. She did not want to look at him. It was the first time in my life I had seen my mother afraid. It was not a good thing to see. I looked at the man and tried to ignore my mother, tried to be tough, like a man should be when someone scares the people he carries inside always. I wanted to hurt this disrespectful man, but then he looked back at me and his eyes turned black, like a…krovoizliyaniye of darkness. Seeing his eyes turn black made me feel very cold inside and out. It was like all the cold, dark nights, all the dangerous animals and hard ice of the taiga lived inside him and he could make me feel that with only a look. I was very scared, okamenela. Bad, bad feeling. I did not hurt the man. I was a coward. I took my mother's arm and walked away. I could hear my mother's prayers and the man's laugh as I walked away. He was the only man I had ever walked away from until now."

The Russian stopped and took a deep breath before continuing.

"I think these men you are having troubles with are like that man. They have made a deal with Tchort and you should not try to mess with them. Go away, ischezat'. Give them what they want. Just get them away from you and keep them away. Nothing good will happen if you go after them. What they have inside, it is not human. You can not kill things that are not human with bullets or knives."

Back to square one. And this time around, I didn't even have a plan.

"I…I don't know what to tell you. I guess I should thank you for looking into this. I didn't know it was going to…turn out this way."

"Temnaya magiya, Nando. This is what these men are into. You don't want to make men that deal with this angry because they can hurt your body and your dusha. Whatever this is about, walk away."

The Russian hung up. I felt lonely and scared. I knew what I had to do, so I got up and walked to my Santa Muerte statue.

I'd left the papers Consuelo had given me next to the statue. I lit up the second candle and read the prayer for the second day of the novena.

Novena a la Santa Muerte
Día 2

Santa Muerte, mi gran tesoro, no te alejes en ninguna ocasión: comiste pan y de él me diste y como Dueña Poderosa de la Negra Mansión, de la existencia y de la vida, Emperatriz de las Tinieblas quiero que me hagas el gran favor de apartar a Indio y a su gente de mi camino, que aquel que me desea mal sufra lo mismo que me desea y que la gente que quiere verme mal tenga que llorar de angustia al verme triunfador. Estos son los favores que humildemente te pido, esperando que se cumpla a la mayor brevedad. Que así sea.

Praying helped a bit, just like it always did, but knowing that I had to get dressed and go talk to Guillermo again was making me feel like I'd swallowed a few razor blades. Knowing that I'd see Consuelo again and could ask her for a stronger limpia was not enough to make me feel better.

9

Fantasmas and bullets
Jacketed hollow-points – Sicarios
Heavy – Solid – Black
Cow tongue

Talking to Guillermo and telling him the Russian had declined the job would only go smoothly if I had an alternate plan. I needed to come up with that plan. And a gun. A big gun with some balas de plata. Y cojones. Muchos cojones.

I had no idea where I could get massive cojones, but the gun was another story. I swiped my finger across my phone's screen and dialed Ricky's Bike Shop.

Ricky was a skinny güey with long blonde dreadlocks and a patchy blonde beard who ran a bicycle chop shop. Drove a blue Prius with too many bumper stickers, all about yoga, coexisting, and eating vegetables instead of meat. He came from Portland, where he'd been caught too many times, and had set up business in Austin because the city, like Portland, had an incredible amount of assholes willing to pay top dollar for stolen bikes instead of driving a car like a regular person. Save the planet, but fuck your neighbor. Typical white mierda. Since the bike business wasn't enough to pay for the Vegas trips and weekend-long benders Ricky enjoyed, he sold guns on the side. Bikes paid for his rent and occasional meals, but the pistolas paid for the things he loved: booze, blow, and blowjobs.

He picked up on the third ring.

"Ricky's Bike Shop. Ricky speaking. How may I help you?"

"Hey, Ricky, it's Fernando."

"Hey, what up, ese?"

Ricky had a thing for slang. White, brown, black, whatever. His personality was like the sails of a boat and obeyed whatever breeze was flowing at any given time. I wasn't sure if that made him a pinche pendejo or very dangerous. I always treated him well just in case it was the latter. After all, he had all the pistolas in the world.

"I need something, man. I lost the last bike I got from you."

"You lost it? How can you lose such a thing, ese?"

"Well, it was stolen."

Ricky laughed. I hadn't said anything funny, but whatever. Algunos pinches gringos se ríen por todo.

"No worries, man. I actually have something you might really dig. Got it the other day and remembered your tattoos and shit. No one has jumped on it, so it's yours if you want it. I can give you a sweet deal on it. You ever seen *The Boondock Saints*?"

"No."

"Oh, man, it's a pretty sweet flick. You have to see it. Anyway, get your brown ass down here and I'll explain it to you. That little taco truck around the corner is already spitting smoke, so we can grab some food and talk business. Shop is dead, anyway."

"Okay, I'll be there in a few."

I hung up and thought about taking a Xanax along with the Oxy my mind was craving. However, I wanted to be a little sharper than that for my visit to Ricky. I wanted to make sure that I went in there, got a gun, and left without having to put up with three hours of the man talking nonsense and asking questions. My brain needed the fluffy coating of something, but not too much. Thoughts of Indio had to be kept on a soft pillow inside my head or their sharpness would tumble around and destroy everything, but getting zombified was not an option, so the Oxy went down my throat alone.

Ricky was blasting some death metal when I showed up. It sounded like a buffalo stampede passing through a drum shop. I always thought he looked like a reggae kind of guy, but I guess loud screaming and distortion kept him happy.

He turned the racket down as soon as he saw me.

"What up, ese? Shut the door behind you."

I threw the lock and flipped the sign to CLOSED.

"How you doing, Ricky?"

"I'm good, bro, I'm good."

Ricky came around the counter, his yellow dreadlocks swinging all over the place, and gave me a hug. He always did that. With everyone. I had no doubt he would shoot me in the head if someone offered him fifty bucks or un cuarto de coca.

"So you have something for me?"

If I didn't keep Ricky focused, he'd start talking about his last bender, snorting lines off a stripper's culo or how it was increasingly harder to keep up with the demand for top-notch lowrider bikes. He thought that me being Mexican meant I was tight with the cholos that fucked around with cars and bikes all over town.

"Sure do, bro. Follow me."

Ricky walked around the counter and opened a door that lead to the real office, the secret garage in the back where bikes came in and became something new. Parts and wheels hung from the ceiling and the walls and there were half-constructed bikes all over the place. Ricky walked to a huge red toolbox that was almost as tall as me. He opened one of the bottom drawers and pulled out a black gun. He looked at the piece with a smile on his face and handed it to me.

It was heavy. Solid. All black. I was never a fan of guns, but this was the first gun I'd touched since having the pinches mareros steal my old piece, and it felt good.

"That's a Beretta 92SF. You already know 9mms are awesome, but this is top of the line, man, this thing comes fucking loaded. Three-dot sighting system, super reliable open slide design, safety-decocking lever on both sides, and a really sweet and easy to use mag-release mechanism that you can switch around if you want to. Oh, and you can keep this thing in your fucking gym bag and it won't corrode or anything. Super sweet gun, man."

Ricky talked about bikes and guns the way teenage boys talk about tits. He was excited about what he was showing me. I just wanted a gun that wouldn't lock up on me. While he rattled on and on about the gun, I turned it over and pretended to be studying it. On the left side it said PIETRO BERETTA and then, in smaller letters, GARDONE V.T.-MADE IN ITALY. Just below that, I found what I was looking for. Instead of the serial number, there was a slightly discolored triangle that someone had tried really hard to disguise via polishing. This thing looked brand new, but it could have a few bodies on it already. I didn't care. My plans included adding a few bodies to its list.

The Oxy was kicking in. I felt like I wanted to take a nap. It was time to speed things up.

"Bullets?"

"No, no, no. Wait a minute, man. Remember I asked you if you had seen *The Boondock Saints*?"

"Yeah."

"Well, this was the gun they used. As soon as I got it, I thought about your ink!"

Ricky was talking about the Virgen de Guadalupe, which occupied my left forearm, and the Santa Muerte con su guadaña, which was on my right bicep. La virgencita I got because my mom would always give me her bendiciones whenever I left the house and, once I started spending more time on the streets than in my house, I felt like I needed those bendiciones. La Niña Blanca I got my first year in Austin. It was my way of thanking her for helping me stay alive and a way to carry her with me wherever I went. It had been done by Elisa, a woman who worked at Fantastic Tattoo and who claimed ángeles lived in her shop and guided her hand while she worked. She was the second person I planned on seeing that day. That would only happen if I managed to escape Ricky's shop before Elisa went home for the day.

"Thanks for thinking about me, Ricky. Means a lot."

I didn't.

"How much do you want for it and can you give me some bullets?"

"Listen, bro, I'd ask anyone else for $500, but since they stole your piece, give me $400 and it's yours. Also, I'm gonna give you some special bullets. Check this out."

Ricky turned around, walked back to the toolbox, and opened a different drawer. He came back holding a dark blue box. With a huge smile on his thin lips, Ricky shook his dreadlocks back over his shoulder and held the box up as if he'd suddenly became one of those nice ladies whose sole job is to show contestants shit at game shows. Fiocchi ammunition. 9mm luger. 115 GRS. JHP.

"You see these babies?"

"Yeah."

"See that JHP at the bottom?"

"Yep."

Ricky brought the box down and looked at me as if I'd missed a hilarious joke.

"Jacketed hollow-points, bro. This shit will do some major damage."

Jacketed hollow-points. I'd never seen them before. A lot of sicarios who worked for the carteles liked these bullets. Instead of entering someone and flying out of them on the other side, these thing opened up like a metallic flower on impact, causing a hell of a lot of carnage and blood loss. Usually I wouldn't see the need to load my gun with balas like that, but with the smile on Indio's face as he sawed off Nestor's head burned into the back of my eyelids forever, they struck me as the perfect thing.

"Are they really hollow?"

"Yeah, bro, I wouldn't lie to you, you know that."

My question had nothing to do with Ricky's honesty, but what I had in mind was not something I was willing to discuss with him.

"Cool, man. I'll take them."

The cash came out and Ricky's eyes lit up. I counted twenty twenties. The green was down his pocket so quick I didn't even see it. He handed me the box of balas, a 15 round mag, and patted me on the arm.

"Shit, ese, I wouldn't want to be the guy who stole your piece right now!"

"They took more than my gun."

"So you're buying this thing just to get your stuff back? For some payback?"

"No, I'm buying this to make sure those hijueputas don't ever steal anything from anyone ever again."

Apparently my words carried some odio in them because the smile on Ricky's face died quicker than a cockroach under a fat man's boot.

"So…how bout those tacos now?"

I hadn't had anything to eat, so I nodded despite the fact that having lunch with Ricky was not something I'd normally do. It's hard to enjoy your tacos when some pinche gringo is going on and on about the latest stripper he banged.

"Cool, man, cool! Let's head out. I'm starving. Oh, hey, do you guys really eat cow tongue?"

Sometimes the best thing that happens to other people is an unloaded gun.

10

Cold, sharp silence
La huesuda – Missing chingos – Blood
San Lázaro – Snake around my lungs
Pain

I drove to Guillermo's house in a blur. I parked the car more or less in the same spot I'd parked the previous day and sat there, suddenly remembering the cracked egg and its nasty, slithering contents. I felt like I now had some of those worms crawling around my soul.

I shut the car off and stepped down. I was walking up to the door when I remembered to text Guillermo.

I'm here again. Need to talk.

Then I waited.

After five minutes or so, I decided to give him a call. It was too damn hot to be waiting on the sidewalk and my car was surely approaching sauna temperatures, so sitting and waiting in it was out of the question.

The damn phone rang until it went to voicemail. I tried again. Same result.

Guillermo's car was in the driveway. I decided to knock and deal with the dogs then and Guillermo's anger later.

I walked up to the door and knocked. Silence.

I knocked again. Silence again.

I knocked harder and faster, calling out Guillermo's name.

Nothing.

I then repeated the process but called out to Consuelo instead.

Nada.

Sin pensarlo, I grabbed the doorknob and twisted. The door was open. I pushed it in slowly, expecting a dog to jump out at me at any moment, despite the silence. I peeked inside and saw an empty living room. No one stood in the kitchen. No barking and no music. El silencio tenía filo.

I pushed the door open un poco más and then stopped. There was a pool of blood coming from the kitchen and covering half of the hallway's floor. Every muscle on my body wanted to jump back, slam the door, get in my car, and haul ass out of there.

Consuelo.

I pulled the nine and stepped in. Gun raised.

Something fast, invisible, and cold slammed against me and then went through me, taking the air in my lungs with it.

La huesuda.

El aire se escapó de mis pulmones tan rápido como si hubiése visto al diablo. I knew immediately that la huesuda had been in the house and had left, going through me on her way out. Se me puso la piel de gallina.

Por favor, mi querida Niña Blanca, mi Santísima Muerte, gran potectora, no me abandones ahora.

I took a few steps forward on wobbly legs, breathing as if I'd just ran a marathon in the mud while carrying someone on my back.

The blood coming from the kitchen hadn't turned completely black yet. That meant la huesuda had stuck around, fed off whatever evil had been there.

I heard screams that weren't there and felt a cold that was impossible given the heat I'd felt outside, but still I walked toward the blood.

Not wanting to step on the brownish puddle, I decided to walk up to the counter and lean over it to look into the kitchen. I lead with the pistol.

Mi corazón had already stopped beating a few seconds before I saw Consuelo's lifeless body sitting on the floor, her back against the cabinet door under the kitchen sink. Algo me apretaba el pecho y no me dejaba respirar. Air and tears came simultaneously, my gulping for air drowning the scream that had built up in my throat and was threatening to come out and obliterate everything around me.

I forgot about the puddle and my own safety and jumped over the counter to reach Consuelo. I placed the pistol on the counter and kneeled next to her and touched her shoulder. Her head rolled to the left, exposing the gash on her neck. Someone had slashed her throat so viciously it had almost severed her head.

Something snapped inside of me, something untouchable that would never be put together again.

I wanted to grab Consuelo's head and put her back together somehow. I wanted her to look up at me and tell me to call for help. I wanted to find the person who had done this. I wanted to scream, to burn something, to reach inside myself and pull out the cold stone that was sitting at the bottom of my stomach and the serpiente that had curled around my lungs. I wanted to murder and destroy and cry and turn to dust so I could forget everything, abandon the pain, and fly away.

Quería todo a la vez y no quería absolutamente nada.

My body was shaking and snot was coming out of my nose faster than the tears that came from my eyes. Consuelo was gone. Para siempre.

La huesuda se me antojó en ese momento una puta mala, una inútil, una pinche malnacida.

I stood up and picked up the gun and walked to the hallway, slipping for a second on the congealing blood. I reached out and touched the wall of that cursed house to catch myself. If whoever had done this was still in the house, I was going to rip their chest open with my hands and eat their fucking heart while they were still twitching on the floor.

I walked down the hallway and looked into the bathroom and the first room. The bathroom only had Consuelo's collection of perpetually-burning candles in the tub and the room only housed her bed, an old rocking chair, and a gigantic statue of San Lázaro surrounded by a pack of dogs that were licking the wounds on his legs.

I finally reached the room that more or less acted as Guillermo's office and found him on the floor. His body, which was between the sofa and the coffee table, was covered in blood and bloodied one-dollar bills. In the crook of his left arm sat the headless corpse of a brown chicken. Two blue candles had burned themselves out on the table, their wax mixing together to form a hard puddle. Guillermo's head sat on the chair where the Niño Fidencio guayabera hung. The candle underneath the chair had been extinguished. The room smelled like death and shit.

I knew almost nothing about santería, vudú y palo mayombe, but I'd been around enough santeros and paleros to know that someone had performed a ritual to get money. Consuelo dead and Guillermo's head sitting in a chair because of pinche lana. The anger inside me grew even more. It grew so much I thought it was going to rip my chest apart.

Indio.

"Ogún oko dara obaniché aguanile ichegún iré."

Clear. Sharp.

"Ogún oko dara obaniché aguanile ichegún iré."

I felt those words would come together and help some evil presence materialize.

The thought slithered its way into my brain, as full of venom as it was full of truth. This was my fault.

Indio had picked me to deliver a message. He knew what he'd done was not a matter that could be discussed over the phone. I led them here.

Ser marioneta es tan malo como ser un chivato.

The blood was already on the floor. Las almas ya habían partido.

Lo peor de la muerte es lo que le hace a los vivos.

Consuelo was dead because of me.

I vomited. Then, with the taste of bile and snot coating the inside of my mouth, a second thought came and made the guilt lose all its devastating sharpness. I was a witness. I knew who had done this. I could tell anyone. Guillermo's brother could, and probably would, ask me if I knew anything. I'd served my purpose and was now a liability, a loose end, a small aggravation on two legs that would have to be taken care of.

Sometimes darkness gets so close you can feel it touching your skin, pushing against your innards like a brutal magnetic force. I felt it. Sentí una oscuridad tan absoluta, una maldad tan profunda acechándome, que caí de rodillas. There, brought to my knees like a beaten fighter, my head against the wall and my thoughts spinning out of control like a big rock rolling down a very steep hill, I heard a voice.

"Levántate, mijo."

That was all I needed.

Consuelo was still around. Her strength was my strength. I walked back to her body.

Some people are pura luz.

The day I met her came back to me as I looked down at the deep, red wound splitting her neck.

On that first day, she gave me a hug before I left, told me I was un hijo de Changó.

"Mijo, tu eres hijo Changó, el hijo de Ibaíbo y Yemmú, el patrón de los guerreros y las tempestades."

I told her I was a devout of Santa Muerte, but she told me it didn't matter. She knew Shangó was both looking out for me and putting dangerous obstacles in my way. "Give me a few weeks, mijo, and I'll figure out why."

We never talked about that again.

Consuelo was an enmantillada, someone who was born inside the amniotic sac and thus possessed the gift of sight beyond all veils, trough all smoke, and into the minds of people.

Now her luz was gone. Bad death and bad vibes. The same things were inside me. I needed to change that. Someone needed to pray for Consuelo and Guillermo to make sure their almas didn't turn into espíritus vagabundos.

I kneeled next to Consuelo and prayed a few Padre Nuestros for them and asked Santa Muerte to lead them to a better place quickly. Then I got up, placed the plug on the kitchen sink, and ran the faucet. I threw some water on the counter and used the sponge on the sink to wipe away any possible fingerprints. The water would take care of the mess I'd made up and down the hallway.

I kissed Consuelo's grey head and went back to Guillermo. I stepped over him without looking and grabbed Niño Fidencio's shirt and threw it over my shoulder. If el Niño Fidencio was really a milagrero, I was going to give him a chance to throw a milagro my way.

I went to Consuelo's room and picked up her San Lázaro statue, heavy as an overpacked suitcase.

I walked into the kitchen again and realized I'd been crying since I before I started praying. I placed the San Lázaro statue on the counter so it wouldn't get any blood on it and kneeled once more. I closed my eyes and placed one last kiss on Consuelo's head. That kiss said thank you and have a safe journey and rest in peace and te amo with no words. Then, with my lips still buried in her gray hair, I made a promise out loud so that even the fantasmas that weren't listening to my kiss could hear it.

"Te voy a vengar."

I got up, picked up the statue, and left the house, already knowing what I'd do the second I got home.

11

Oración desesperada
Synov'ya sukin
Angry Russian – Bad ideas
The Dyatlov boys

The first thing I did when I got home was place my new statue next to Santa Muerte and pray.

Santisíma Muerte, hoy vengo a ti de rodillas y con lágrimas en los ojos para pedirte un gran favor con todo mi corazón: que me protejas de mis enemigos y de sus malas intenciones y que ayudes a Consuelo y a Guillermo a entrar para siempre en la gloria del Señor. Hoy te ruego que me mires con ojos de piedad y que perdones mis faltas y me ayudes a que las mismas sean perdonadas por el Dios Todopoderoso. Igualmente te pido que me sanes de toda enfermedad natural y sobrenatural, que me protejas del mentiroso, del envidioso, del malvado, del traidor y de las malas energías y los malos espíritus. Por favor concédeme tu justicia en todo momento y protégeme de aquellos que me desean sólo daños y mal. Concédeme tus bendiciones y tus milagros y otorgame las bendiciones de tu diestra poderosa hoy siempre.

Next up were some phone calls.

I thought about calling Raúl and asking him for help, but he was going to ask a lot of questions and, if

I told him the real story, he would probably place the blame on me. And he'd be right. At least un poquito.

This was my problem, and I had enough anger and pain inside me to accept that.

And I had my gun.

With my eyes on my new statue, I pulled out my phone and dialed.

"Ved'ma Nursery, how may I help you?"

"Hey, man, it's Fernando."

The Russian waited a few seconds and then replied.

"Nando, it is good to hear from you. How can I help you now? I hope this is not about our last conversation."

"It is about our last conversation, but I don't want you to do anything for me other than tell me how you found the men."

"Nyet, Nando. I told you to drop this, to ischezat', to go somewhere else. No more business with these men for me. You should do the same."

"They killed Guillermo and Consuelo."

This time I was expecting the pause. It came accompanied by a sigh.

"Synov'ya sukin. I didn't like the fat man much, he was lazy and expected too many favors from people, but he didn't deserve to die, not at the hands of these sviney. And the mysterious woman who lived with him, I have heard stories. She was a true ved'ma, a providets. These people, they are special. My grandmother was one. Only fucking cowards kill women. I hope her prizrak moves into their bad dreams forever."

"I need to know where I can find them."

"My friend, Guillermo and the woman, they were not your sem'ya, not of your blood. I don't think killing yourself is the way to deal with the pain. It won't bring them back. I understand mest'. It is my business. Maybe you can find someone else to take care of it, but you are in much danger if you try to do it yourself. Trust me. I have seen these bad men with my own eyes, remember? They have evil inside."

"I came to this country running from men like them, men who killed my friends and wanted me dead. I will have to run again if I don't kill them. I don't want to run. I'm tired of running. I'm sick of living like a coward, of feeling like a coward, of…"

"You are young, Nando, the anger, it bends you to its will. Going after these men is a bad idea, but I can see that my words will not stop you. I understand that. The fear, it is more powerful than the anger. You are feeling both. That is enough to make anyone bezumnyy."

"So would you please let me know where I can find Indio?"

"Yes, this I will do. My hope is that your angel-khranitel' is strong. Very, very strong. Your death, it is not something I want on my back. Carrying ghosts around is very bad for your dusha.

"My friend Igor Dyatlov, he has a small food store on the east side, near Rosewood Park. His wife Lyuda manages a few molodezh' that sell weed and pills for them near the park. They are good people, chestnyy. They see thing clearly and do straight business with everyone. I always ask them whenever I have to find someone in the city. Most of the time they can't help, but sometimes they have something for me because they have eyes many places in the east side. This time they were able to help me very much. The men you want to find have been pushing, nazhav, themselves into most of the business in the parks on the other side of I-35. They beat up two of the Dyatlov boys. Igor and Lyuda are angry, so they were very quick to share the information with me. After that, I only had to drive around for a few hours to find them. No trouble. I spotted them in a blue car leaving Webberville Road. I followed them for a while. They bought food from a truck on Airport Boulevard and then went back to a house in Webberville, a rushitsya place behind T.B.'s Lounge. They hung out outside and smoked. I drove by. That's when I saw the man with the tattoos in the face. He looked back at me and his eyes, they turned black."

I knew where T.B.'s Lounge was. I knew T.B., an old black man who ran the prostitution and gambling joints in a chunk of the east side. Was he helping out the mareros?

"Thank you for the information, man."

I expected The Russian to hang up. Instead, he asked me a question.

"You will go after these men, yes?"

"I will. I'm really hoping I don't have to do it alone, but going after them is the plan."

"You will do me a favor?"

"Yes. I owe you that and more."

"If you get to them and you survive, you will call me and let me know that men who have made deals with Tchort can bleed. Mozhet Gospod's vami."

The click I'd expected earlier now surprised me.

12
Invisible hammer
Una venganza certera y sangrienta
New ink – Skinny bearded saint
Cojones de buey

What happens sometimes is that life resembles a porn movie. You tell yourself that you like what you see, but it takes a lot of effort to keep at it. You think about beauty and try to use an invisible hammer to make what you're looking at sort of fit into the hole created by your ideals. The lie works for a while, but then you start seeing truth; you start spotting the acne on the guy's back and the thin dark scars under the woman's breasts and you realize he's holding his dick in his fist like he's trying to make the head pop because he's so damn high he has to look down to see planes and can't get hard. That's when the lie crumbles like a deck of cards in a hurricane. Suddenly her fake screaming and moaning starts getting on your nerves, like when two cats fight outside your window at three in the morning and the loser stays there after the action is over, wailing away like a banshee.

What happens then is that sadness creeps in, dragging shame along like a beaten dog with a filthy chew toy in its mouth. Yeah, the lie is gone and all you're left with is a black hole where your heart used to be and a limp dick in your hand. What happens once the castle of lies you call a life is gone is that a desire to escape builds up inside you and sours everything you do, taints everything you experience, sucks the color out of everything you see.

Our lives aren't as great as we want to believe they are, and being afraid is a magnifying glass that makes you see every painful detail, every crack.

What happens when you accept that the lie is over is that you have to change things or ignore them.

What happens when someone takes someone you love away from you is that your lie crumbles but you also fall into a hole and start hating the walls around you. That hate eats you up like a cancer and the only cure es una venganza certera y sangrienta. Action. Don't let anyone feed you any bullshit when it comes to venganza because something that feels so good, so right, tan cósmicamente correcto, is something that can't be wrong.

The bad thing about that venganza is that you need inner strength to make it happen. Necesitas cojones de buey.

What happens when you decided to act, when you decided to make things right, is that you go out and get a gun. Then you go to a tattoo place with a picture of a San Lázaro statue on your phone and you show it to the artist. Then you sit around and wait for a while. Eventually, the artist comes to you with a smaller version of the saint, a version small enough to fit on your forearm. You nod. Then comes the shaving and the placing of the stencil and the needle with its endless buzzing that mixes with the pills you took and places your brain somewhere between this world and the world of dreams.

The skinny bearded holy man on your forearm is surrounded by dogs. That puts a small smile on your face. You thank the artist and leave a hundred-dollar tip because the ink makes you feel powerful and protected and your endorphins are working tiny miracles as they mix with the other chemicals in your bloodstream. You wish you could bottle that feeling and carry it with you wherever you go.

What happens next is, you think you have a plan. That plan is simple, but simple is almost always the opposite of easy.

What happens when you have a plan but you're not sure about it is that you realize you have to ask someone about it, and when the person you usually consult about such things is no longer in this realm, you have to concentrate to find a viable alternative.

That's when you remember a man Consuelo told you about, a man whom she said could see even farther than she could and never blinked.

13
Visita al visionero
The motherfucker doesn't blink
The bones never lie – Cards
Castle in the distance

I drove north on North Lamar and kept an eye out for the big red neon hand like los tres reyes magos kept an eye out for that guiding star.

Ten minutes later I spotted the place, did a U-turn, and parked.

The place had no name. It was one-story building with a façade made of light brown rocks. A giant red neon palm decorated the front. The words PALM READINGS and TAROT READINGS shone the same neon red on either side of the palm. The door was painted purple and had an OPEN sign hanging from the doorknob.

Memories of driving Consuelo there invaded my head. She wanted to know if someone had done a trabajo on her dead sister and was curious about her health in the upcoming months because she'd been feeling tired. I asked her why she went to see this guy when it was obvious she could she beyond the veil. "You can see others very well, Nando, but your reflection always comes at you twisted regardless of the quality of the mirror," she'd said.

Not wanting to let the memories mess me up, I stepped out of my car and walked into the place. A skinny man who looked seven feet tall sat on a purple stool in the middle of an empty room. The only illumination in the room came from a collection of candles surrounding the room, all of them pressed against the walls. The gaunt man stood up and looked at me. I remembered then what Consuelo called him when she asked me to bring her there, "the man with wild eyes and many faces." His eyes looked normal to me.

Then I remembered she'd said he never blinked.

The man walked toward me slowly. He wore black jeans and a blue shirt with a purple vest. Every finger had a ring and necklaces made of beads of every color known to man hung from his neck. His arms were covered with tatuajes of faces, numbers, and names. I didn't recognize any of the faces, but some of the names I saw were familiar. Blavatsky. Crowley. Laveau. Boukman. The portions of his neck that were not covered by the necklaces were also covered with small, intricate designs. Some were numbers in a line and some resembled the drawings voodoo practitioners use in their incantations and rituals.

Maybe it was because my spirits were down or maybe because Consuelo had spoken so highly of this man, but he struck me as someone with incredible power.

When the man reached me, he said "Welcome," and stuck out his hand. His voice sounded like dust being scraped off an old wooden surface. I took his hand.

He squeezed my fingers with the strength of a man four times his size. I felt weak compared to him, small despite outweighing him by at least 80 pounds.

"I'm sorry for your loss," he said with that voz de ultratumba. He sounded sincere.

I kept quiet.

"You're lost. You have suffered a great loss and now love and hate are fighting inside you. When the sons and daughters of Changó get lost, they either disappear or learn to wield the power of their Father. Which group do you belong to, my friend?"

"I think I belong to the second group. That's why I came to see you..."

"Isaac," he said.

"Isaac, I came here because Consuelo said..."

"Consuelo," he said, giving my hand one more squeeze and then letting it go with the same care one puts down a newborn baby. "She's the hole in your heart. That space is full of negative energy now. The weight of it is making breathing difficult, but don't despair, her light is keeping absolute darkness and an eternal storm of pain and bone dust from sweeping you away. She has left this plane, but her enlightened spirit is no longer bound to inaction by the limits imposed on us by flesh. She's far more powerful now than she ever was, and that is a beautiful thing. I very much look forward to her visit."

He stopped talking and looked at a spot behind me. His lips curled up into something akin to a smile, but it immediately vanished. I kept my eyes glued to his, but he didn't blink.

"Consuelo is with you, protecting you now and in the trip you're about to embark on. Be careful in this endeavor. The world of eternal danger and sharp shadows is trying to invade you. She can't protect you if you don't do your part."

"I want to go aft…"

He raised his right hand with a quickness that seemed impossible given the calm look on his skeletal face.

"You are a blind man trapped in a boat with no captain in the middle of an uncharted ocean. I'll ask the Orishas. Come with me."

He turned around and used one incredibly long arm to part the beaded doorway to the side. A small round table with a white cloth and two chairs stood in the middle of the room.

Isaac produced a deck of tarot cards.

"Pick three cards. Don't look at them. Hold them by your side and imagine them gone. We will do something else first."

I did what he asked me to. Isaac nodded and wrapped the remaining cards in a blue handkerchief.

I thought we were going to sit down, but he turned and led me out of the room. About a third of the candles had blown out in the very short time we spent in the tiny room and everything looked darker now. We walked behind the black curtain entered a small room with no furniture. The walls looked like they had been painted with blood using a hand instead of a brush. The skin of some brown animal was laid out on the floor. Next to it was a small vase made of mud.

Isaac bent down and picked up the vase. He looked

at me and started shaking it. A few seconds later, he tipped the contents on top of the animal skin. I looked down. About twenty little bones were sprawled over the skin. Some looked like chicken neck bones but others were larger and I couldn't imagine what kind of animal they came from. At least two of them looked like tiny penises. I was sure those came from human fingers. Issac kneeled down and studied the bones for a while. I kept my mouth shut. He started speaking without removing his eyes from the bones.

"Death has been a part of your life for a long time, but the death that's breathing down your neck now is a different beast. A son of Ogún has crossed your path. The many sacrifices this man has made to his Father have made the god hungry for more. Ogún wants your blood. 'Ogún shoro shoro, eyebale kawo.' He speaks loudly through blood and killing. This man has a dark pact, an unhealthy understanding with Ogún."

When a man wants you dead, you think about killing him first, about being smarter and faster and putting a few holes in his body before he can catch you slippin', but what the hell are you supposed to do when a god wants you dead?

"The bones never lie. They have knowledge that precedes us and all of our religions. They're inhabited by spirits from Africa that witnessed the birth of our gods and feasted on their afterbirth. Trust what they say. They say you are a lucky man. Changó is your Father. He doesn't want you dead, much less at the hands of a son of Ogún. However, Changó's good will and Consuelo's light might not be enough if you don't make an effort to fight. The matters of the Orishas are complicated when they are carried by the hands of men. These men are drunk on blood and power. They are ignoring Ogún's cries for blood, plying their bodies with liquor and chemicals. This has upset their god. Which is good for you."

"I'm praying a novena to Santa Muerte," I said. "I burn a candle for her every day and offer her rum and food."

"That's good. Burn a few candles for Changó as well. Offer him white wine and apples. These things will keep him happy and watching over you. Now show me your cards."

I had forgotten about the cards. I turned them over and held them in front of me like a kid holds an unknown insect.

The first card showed a tower being struck by lightning. People were jumping out of windows into a starless night.

"The Tower," said Isaac. "Turmoil. Life's rug is being pulled from under your feet. You're falling, scared and confused. Something is striking down on you with a ferocious force. When life is a mess, a devastating fire is needed to clear out the dead wood, to scare bad creatures away, to clear the space and strengthen the soil so that fresh seedlings can sprout, take root. Survival is the only path to strength and vice versa."

Isaac removed the Tower card from between my fingers and looked at the second card. A woman with a blindfold on and her arms tied behind her back stood among very tall swords stuck in the earth. Behind her, a castle rose up in the distance at the top of a mountain.

"The Eight of Swords," said Isaac. "Oppression. The castle, the oppressive force, it watches over your every action. The woman looks trapped, helpless, but her feet are not tied. She's free to run, or to a use a sword to cut the binds from her hands and face her oppressor. The choice is yours."

Once again, Isaac plucked the card he'd been reading from between my fingers and looked at the card that was behind it. It showed a skeleton riding a white horse and holding a strange flag. A dead man was underneath the horse and a couple of kids were in front of it. One seemed to be dying and the other one looked like he was praying.

"Whispers from the future. Death. An intense change is at hand, a transmutation that requires action. The nature of Death is duality. The meaning of this card is in your hands. Obey the Orishas and Death can be a commanding force that carries you into a new plane. Disobey and the dark forces around you swallow you whole. Death of the flesh is only one of many."

I needed to get out that small room with its bloody walls and the man who never blinked.

"How much do I owe you?"

"A friend of Consuelo would never owe me anything. Take what you have learned and use it. Retribution feels personal, but it can be a communal event. Keep that in mind as you move forward. Burn your candles. Offer Changó some apples. Let him know that you acknowledge his power. Be humble. Pray every day to your Santa Muerte. She is a good protector and healer. Give her a soul to deliver. Whether that soul is yours or someone else's is entirely up to you."

He was done. He raised his arm and motioned for me to walk out.

I mumbled another thank you and reached the door in a few hurried steps.

As I reached the door, I turned one last time to look at the man who never blinked. His feet were hovering about two inches from the floor.

14
Butterflies are sometimes dragonflies
Monstruos that hide in the sombras
Late night visit – Licking flesh
Tears

With my new gun tight against the small of my back I went to work. If they wanted to come for me, I was ready. I thought back to what the unblinking man had said. They were getting confident. Sloppy. Drunk on their power. I stood a few feet away from the doorway, checked IDs, and placed whatever drug people asked for in their hands with practiced disimulo.

I also ignored my phone. Surely some of the calls had to be from someone asking about Guillermo. He rarely left the house, but he was good about picking up his phone. I hoped no one had needed him too desperately. I needed time.

Once things had fallen into their mid-night rhythm, I went to the back and talked to Manny, a Mexican American mountain of blubber and attitude who sucked as a bartender but was good with the money box. Manny had a black girlfriend who worked at one of T.B.'s strip clubs. She went by Butterfly despite the fact that the huge insect tattooed between her ridiculously huge fake tits was a dragonfly. I knew Butterfly was

133

tight with Nikki and Baby Girl, the two young ladies who ran everything while T.B. pretended he was the man of the house. If T.B. had anything to do with the men living in the tiny house behind his juke joint, these ladies would know about it, and they would tell Butterfly what was up.

As awful as Manny was to almost everyone, he had this twisted idea that, since I was the one who placed all the money in the box he got paid to protect with his life, he was supposed to keep me happy because I was above him in pay and rank. I never had time, or the desire, to explain to him he was wrong. If his confusion kept his huge ass docile and hasta un poco servicial, so be it.

It didn't take long. Manny tapped me on the shoulder about an hour before closing. T.B. was clean. According to Manny, the "tattooed motherfuckers" had even gone to one T.B.'s clubs, harassed a few dancers, and then stabbed a bouncer with a broken bottle when he tried to kick them out.

That sucked for the dancers and the bouncer, but it was good news for me. The last thing I wanted was to go after Indio and then have the Pussy King, which is what some folks called T.B., coming after me with an army of angry black dudes armed to the teeth.

A few hours later, we pushed the last drunks out into the night and closed up. I walked to my car with the hair on the back of my neck standing up like a cat's and drove home, convinced there was a big brown car following me.

I parked in my usual spot, near some dumpsters, and walked to my door with ears and eyes at attention.

Going home felt like a mistake. I wondered if I was welcoming them, hoping they'd get me like they got me the first time. If they'd just end it. I entered my apartment and closed the door with a sigh of relief.

I got a glass of water and opened the cabinet where I kept my collection of pills. I wanted to sleep for a few hours without my brain screaming nonsense at me. Then I heard a noise. A scratch. Something was scratching at my door.

The gun was in my hand and the safety was off before my brain even had a chance to think about what the noise could be.

Then came a bark.

I walked to the door and listened before putting my eye to the peephole. Loud breathing. Shuffling. If Indio had come for me or had sent one of his monkeys, they'd be quieter about it. Just in case, I placed my finger around the trigger and held the gun in front of me. If someone with a tattooed face was standing on the other side, they'd get a bullet in the chest before they had a chance to realize the door was open.

Then I pulled the door open.

Kahlúa was sitting in front of my door. I lowered the gun. Behind her, the rest of Consuelo's jauría walked around, their heads down and their noses to the ground. One dog was laid out and appeared to be sleeping.

I stuck my head out. Looked left and right. The dogs were alone. Then I looked down at Kahlúa again. She stood up, moved toward me.

The dog smelled the gun and then her muzzle moved up. Suddenly her rough tongue was on my new tattoo. My first instinct was to pull my hand away, but something held it there. After two licks, Kahlúa sat back down and looked up at me with her human eyes. They were full of tears. A tear rolled down her fur. Then she stood up and started trotting away without looking back. The rest of the chingos were all looking at me. Call me crazy but I swear they collectively gave me a nod before trotting off behind Kahlúa. It felt like a blessing, like a message sent by the beautiful soul I knew was now taking care of me.

15

They came looking for blood
What's good for a saint had to be good for a little devil
Historias de la abuela
Electric worms

Knuckles on my door jolted me awake. The bad thing about pill-induced sleep is that reality has to fight its way into your life slowly. When your brain is surrounded by the soft cloth of magical chemicals, the outside world is like an unwanted interruption that gets locked out, and when it suddenly wants to break in, you end up being scared and confused.

"Hey, Nando, you in there?"

Yoli's voice. It helped get me in motion.

I shook my head, trying hard to get rid of something that couldn't be shaken off.

I pulled my jeans on and walked to the door.

The sun was out. It pierced my eyes and cut into my brain the second I opened the door. Yoli spoke from somewhere inside the glare.

"I came by yesterday, but you weren't here. Some guys were hanging out around your door when I got home from school. They were weird as fuck, so I pretended like I hadn't seen them and went into my

139

place. I don't know what kind of friends you keep, but these dudes looked…unsavory."

Despite the blinding sun, her words sent a shiver down my back. The stuff in my system made the shiver leave a trace that lingered for a few seconds. They had come to tie up a loose end.

"What did they look like?"

My voice came out sounding like I had a dead cat stuck in my throat.

"They had tattoos all over. One was smiling as I came around the corner and his teeth were all framed in gold. The other one was a bit shorter…"

"Did they say anything to you?"

"No, I told you, I went into my place. I had my phone in my hand and pretended to be looking at it. I didn't want them to talk to me. They made me uncomfortable. It's not that they were latinos or anything. It wasn't even the tattoos. You know I have nothing against modified people, it's just…I don't know."

I knew exactly what she meant.

"No, I get what you're saying. They're bad dudes. If you see them again, stay away."

My eyes had adjusted a bit to the sun and I could see Yoli now. She wore a red sleeveless shirt and no makeup. Her leche con chocolate cheeks looked like she'd been caught in a freckle storm without an umbrella.

"Listen, Nando, I know you do more than work at the door of some club. We've been neighbors what, three years now? You don't get your mail. You never walk by the office. You keep the weirdest hours. It's all good, I don't judge you, but I need to know if you have some trouble that's following you home. I live here alone and I don't want men like that walking around here every day."

"You don't have to worry about that, Yoli. Those men won't come back. I promise."

"How can you be so sure?"

"I'm going to have a talk with them tonight. I'll tell them not to come by again. Sounds good?"

"Yeah, sounds great."

There was something sharp in her voice, something only women possess. I have no idea what that thing is, but it can destroy a man if you give it the space to do it.

"Listen, I have to make a few phone calls…"

I brought my hand up to rub some of the sleepiness out of my face. Yoli's hand shot out and she grabbed my forearm, twisted it a bit.

"Nice! It's San Lázaro, right? When did you get it?"

I looked at the tatuaje. Elisa had done a fantastic job. Just like the picture I'd shown her, she'd drawn San Lázaro a little bent, with each hand reaching out to a dog. Now, each hand was reaching down to two dogs. The one to his left was Kahlúa. I recognized her despite that fact that the tattoo was in black and grey. The dog to his left was new to me. It was a female. One look at its short, stubby legs and I knew who it was.

"Yeah," I said, which was pretty stupid but also a lot better than nothing.

"My abuelita used to have a statue of him in her little apartment in the Bronx. She prayed to him every night. I remember being young and coming home from the park with scraped knees and having her sit me down on the sofa and letting her dog come over and lick my wounds. She always said something that was good for a saint had to be good for a little devil."

Her smile had all the power of the sun but didn't blind me. Instead, I wanted to look at it forever, to stay there and just look at her glorious face until everything around us turned to dust except our bodies.

"Sounds like your abuelita was a smart woman."

Yoli let go of my arm. Whatever sharpness had been there before now long gone from both her eyes and her tone.

"She was. I try to make her proud every day."

"I'm sure she is."

"Anyway, I'll let you make those phone calls. And thanks for taking to those guys about not dropping by any more. They were…spooky. I know I sound goofy saying that, but they really were."

She had no idea how spooky they were, and I wasn't about to tell her.

"No problem, Yoli."

She said bye, turned around, and went back to her place. I closed the door and stood there, feeling like small electric worms were crawling under my skin. I looked down at the tatuaje again. It was only ink underneath my skin, but those two new dogs made me feel like I wasn't alone any longer.

16
Broken novena
Propietaria y Reina de las Tinieblas del Mas Allá
Rum – Leftover Pizza – Apples
Talking to Changó

You're supposed to pray your novena for nine consecutive days or it won't work, but sometime you have to do something important before the nine days are over, so you put a little something extra in front of la Santísima Muerte and promise that you will light every candle you owe her.

At least that was my plan.

I grabbed the papers Consuelo had given me, lit up another candle, and read.

Novena a la Santa Muerte
Día 3

Yo te imploro con todo el fervor de mi corazón que, así como Dios te hizo inmortal por ser la Muerte Poderosa, la eterna Propietaria y Reina de las Tinieblas del Mas Allá, que con este gran poder que tienes sobre todos y cada uno de los mortales, hagas que mis enemigos no puedan comer en ninguna mesa, que no puedan sentarse en silla alguna, que no tengan tranquilidad, que no logran conciliar el sueño, y que no se cumplan ninguno de sus nefastos deseos. Santa Muerte, mi adorada Niña Blanca, te pido que obligues a mis enemigos a verse derrotados ante ti, a volverse que humildes y rendidos para que lleguen hasta mis pies y pueda yo ser el brazo de tu eternal y divina justicia. Te ruego, Santa Muerte de mi corazón, que me concedas el favor que te pido en esta novena y que no es otro que me permitas, con tu fuerza y bendita protección, vencer a Indio y los suyos, mi enemigos mortals y alimañas que han dañado a gente buena. Que así sea.

After praying, I lit an extra candle for San Lázaro and another one for Changó. Covering all my bases seemed like a good idea. I didn't have any apples, so I went to the fridge and pulled out the bit of milk I had left, some cheese, and leftover pizza from a few days ago. Then I opened the cabinet under the sink and pulled out my best bottle of rum, the one I used for Santa Muerte, and poured some in a glass.

I placed everything in front of my two statues and told Changó I would get him two bags of apples if he helped me out.

17

El Príncipe
Hold your horses
Hurry up and wait
Pinches asesinos

What I'd told Yoli wasn't a lie. I needed to make a very important phone call. I was going to call El Príncipe.

We talked to each other briefly every time he visited Austin with Raúl. He always asked me about the latest narcocorridos and talked about the latest guys he'd killed. The first time, he gave me his cell phone number and told me to call him if I ever needed anything. "Papi, esto yo lo hago porque gusta, viste, no por porque me haga falta," he had said with a wink.

I hated El Príncipe's approach. Too messy. Demasiado arriesgado. Now, however, he was my only option.

He picked up on the second ring.

"Dímelo."

"Príncipe, es Nando, el que trabaja con Guillermo."

"Nando, ¿qué está pasando, mi pana?"

"Es cuento largo pero la versión corta es que mataron a Guillermo y a Consuelo. Los pinches cabrones que lo hicieron van a venir a por mi si no los pillo yo a ellos primero."

"Wait, wait, wait, párame los caballitos un momento, papi, hold your horses. ¿Mataron a Guillermo? ¿Quién carajo? ¿Raúl lo sabe?"

"No sé si lo sabe, pero quiero resolver esto hoy, ahora. Es mi problema. No le digas nada a Raúl rodavía. Me siento responsable. Si bajas de Dallas y me hechas una mano, te pago cuatro mil dólares que es lo que tengo."

"Papi, yo no quiero tu dinero. Tu sabes que yo jalo gatillo por gusto, cabrón. Además, cuando Raúl se entere, seguro me va a pedir que haga lo mismo que tu estás pensando hacer. Si te sientes culpable es por algo. Yo te ayudo a resolverlo. Dame tu dirección. Maybe I even get some brownie points with the boss for taking care of shit before I'm told to, you know?"

I gave him my address. He said he'd be knocking on my door in less than three hours. He was far from being my favorite person in the world, but knowing that I'd have someone with me who didn't give a fuck about killing those pinches asesinos and was willing to pull the trigger for me for free suddenly made me feel a bit better. I even started thinking that this was something I could pull off. As a bonus, I now knew Raúl wouldn't think for a second I had anything to do with his brother's death. He'd think I was just an angry young man who had decided to dish out justice. He might even like that. Si, eso le iba a gustar bastante. I had one less problem to worry about.

18
Popping oxies
Chilaquilitos – Torta de jamón y pollo – Agua fresca de melón
Bathing bullets
Pslam 83

The trip from Dallas to Austin can take anywhere from two and a half hours to five hours, depending on your luck and the kind of crap you run into on I-35. I prayed El Príncipe didn't run into any trouble. I decided to get some breakfast and then fix up a little something special I'd had in mind since visiting Isaac.

I got dressed, popped two oxies, and grabbed my gun. Then I drove to Arandas, one of my favorite nearby Mexican restaurants, and feasted like it was my last meal. Me pedí unos chilaquilitos, una torta de jamón y pollo, y un agua fresca de melón. Si este resultaba ser el ultimo jalón, por lo menos me iba a agarrar con la panza llena.

After the meal I went home and prepared something special.

I placed my Santa Muerte statue on a big plate and poured water over it. Then I collected that holy water, took the quince balas out of the mag, and dropped them into the water. I went to my room and got my bible, which I rarely used. Psalm 83 was what my abuela told

153

me to pray the first time I came home with a bloody nose. I'd read it a few times since then, and now that I was asking Santa Muerte, San Lázaro, and Changó to protect me, I figured praying to my abuela's god one more time couldn't hurt. In front of the soaking balas, I read the last part of el salmo, which was the portion that really interested me:

Oh Dios mío, ponlos como polvo en remolino;
como paja ante el viento.
Como fuego que consume el bosque,
y como llama que incendia las montañas,
así persíguelos con tu tempestad,
y aterrorízalos con tu torbellino.
Cubre sus rostros de ignominia,
para que busquen tu nombre, oh Señor.
Sean avergonzados y turbados para siempre;
sean humillados y perezcan,
para que sepan que sólo tú, que te llamas el Señor,
eres el Altísimo sobre toda la tierra.

The essence of Santa Muerte would make those balas reach their target, and if that failed, maybe God would be there to pick up the slack. It was time to dry the balas and stick them back in the mag. The next time they left that place, it would be with deadly purpose. All I had to do was sit down, enjoy the softness the two oxies were giving everything around me, and wait for El Príncipe. Then I remembered something else. I went to the room, took my shirt off, and put on Niño Fidencio's shirt.

19
Gold cannon
La Barbie – CPS – Leyva
Five pounds of death
Killing a demon

El Príncipe arrived when the sun was starting to cast sombras.

White shirt. Designer jeans that probably were worth at least half my rent. Gorra plana. A thick gold chain around his neck. A throne pendant that must have weighed at least two pounds. White sneakers that looked like he'd pulled them out of the box before getting in his car. I wondered what he thought of my abuelo shirt. He didn't say anything about it.

He looked happy, free of worries. He hugged me and told me he was really sorry about Consuelo. He didn't say shit about Guillermo. For a man so obsessed with putting bullets in people and buying expensive clothes and jewelry, this motherfucker was mucho más observador than what I thought.

He came into the house with a lot of energy, talking about the drive down to Austin. Anyone who talked to him then would have guessed he was going to a picnic by the river and not to try to kill men I wasn't entirely sure could be killed by regular means.

Between Dallas and Austin, he'd lost the all-Spanish thing and switched to the weird Spanglish he used when he was around his boss. Normally I would have interpreted something like that as being induced by nerves, but his face pushed that thought away from me.

"I'm here, man," he said from my sofa, his eyes dancing between mine and the altar. What he thought of the strange offerings in front of it was beyond me. "Tell me how you want to do this shit, papi, que vine ready pa' jalar gatillo. Chequea."

Without letting me reply to his question first, he pulled his oversized white shirt up and pulled out a blocky gun that should have been peeking out of a hole in a war boat instead of his hands. It was plated in gold.

"Eso no es una pistol, güey, eso es un pinche cañon."

He held it up, looking proud.

"Papi, tu sabes cómo nosotros lo hacemos. This baby right here is a gold-plated Desert Eagle. Shoots fifty caliber bullets. First day I shot this thing, I used one hand and this thing casi me arranca el brazo. Haven't seen what it can do to a body yet, but my guess is it won't be nice."

"Where did you get a fucking gold-plated gun?"

"La Barbie gave it to me. Raúl sent me down to Morelos a couple of weeks ago. The CPS needed some fresh faces to help them deal with a few folks that still don't have things clear in their heads because they went nuts after the Mexican Marines killed Leyva. She's fucking hot, man! We kinda had a thing for a day or two. She showed me a few guns she has that are all pink and shit. Then, on our last day there, she gave me this," he said, moving the gun up and down.

My world at the club was so far removed from the nasty stuff going down in Mexico that I didn't even know Los Zetas were helping out the CPS or that La Barbie had acquired enough power to get folks like Raúl to send her some extra muscle now and then. In more than one way, I was glad I didn't know any of that. My world was here, and I liked it that way. Good money, tacos sabrosos, todas las pastillas que quiero, Consuelo, and few deaths. I knew it would never be the same, but hoped that what I was about to do would help me keep the unbroken parts of what I once had.

I walked over to the sofa and signaled for the cañón. El Príncipe turned it around and placed it on my outstretched hand. The damn thing must have weighed at least five pounds.

"No me digas que esta cosa lleva quince balas…"

"No, tipo, siete," he said.

Seven bullets. That meant he had enough firepower to put down seven rhinos.

"Is this the only thing you're bringing? You might need more than seven balas, güey."

"Tengo una Uzi en el carro, papi," he said, his smile like that of a kid talking about his new bike.

"Una Uzi rosita?"

"Nah, that one's black."

For some reason, he looked at the Santa Muerte statue after he said that. I did the same. I returned the gun and sat down next to him.

The light was coming through the window slanted. It got broken by the blinds and seemed to be cutting into my kitchen, making the fridge look like a zebra

159

from another dimension. The sun drops fast in Texas. It was almost, as the gringos say, show time.

"What are you packing?"

I pulled out my gun and showed it to him.

"Una Beretta," he said. "Nueve milímetros. Classic."

"It's full of hollow points."

"Balas huecas. Nice. That means this shit is serious, papi."

"It is."

"Good. I didn't come here to see your ugly face and your weird fucking shrine over there," he said.

"We should be on the road soon. These guys like to hit the streets and operate at night, so my guess is they will be home when the sun goes down, getting ready. If we get there too late, they'll probably be gone, but if we get there soon after nightfall, I think we're gonna catch them. We'll take your car because they know mine. The pinches mareros are in a house on Webberville, right behind T.B.'s Lounge. He's not in on it. I had Manny check for me. The old bastard is clean. Anyway, we'll drive by a few times. I hope they're there. If they are, we get down. If not, we'll hide somewhere and wait."

"How many dudes are we talking about?"

"Creo que cuatro."

"Four? You made me drive all the way here for four dudes? Nando, you could just walk up to their window and spray them yourself with…"

"No, te necesito."

"Why? Are they all packing AKs or something?"

"If there are four, then there are three of them I more or less don't care about, pero el jefe es un tipo raro. I don't know how shit's going to go down and I feel much better with some backup. ¿Me entiendes?"

"Suenas asustado, tipo."

His voice occupied a strange space between a joke and a very judgmental comment. And he was right. I was scared. Very scared. Más asustado que nunca. Being cuates with a man is one thing, but the relationship you have with someone who's not your friend but seems to be willing to put his culo en la línea de fuego for you is a very different animal. Maybe it was time to come clean and tell El Príncipe a bit more, even though I knew my words could make him leave. Maybe telling him that we were going to kill some men and then maybe try to kill a demon was the honest thing to do.

Maybe not.

La omisión es un pecado liviano.

20
Driving to oblivion
Un pase de perico – Chaos – Red mists
The plan that wasn't really a plan
Into the arms of Santa Muerte

El Príncipe's ride was a huge white Escalade. Against all odds, he didn't have that monster sitting on 22s or shooting lights from underneath like he had run over an entire club.

He hit the alarm and then looked around. Instead of opening the driver's door, he walked to the back of the car and opened the trunk. He looked around the parking lot again and then took off his shirt. He wore a white camisilla underneath. He reached into the trunk and pulled out a back bulletproof vest.

"Got this off a cop who owes me a few favors. You got one?"

"No."

"Puñeta, brother, tu eres el tipo más bravo que conozco o el más pendejo."

I was sure it was the latter.

He strapped the vest on and then put his shirt back on.

We climbed into the massive vehicle and the radio exploded to life the second he turned the key in the

165

ignition. Reggaetón. The bass was so loud it made my chest shake. He turned it off. I looked at him.

"They'd hear us coming from a mile away, papi."

I was so worried about what we were going to do that I wasn't thinking straight. Suddenly having El Príncipe conmigo made me feel like that ángel guardián had finally come down from heaven to watch over me. The white shirt and clean face were helping.

El Príncipe knew Webberville. He left my apartment and got on North Loop. We drove straight to Airport and got on it. The moment we passed underneath I-35, my heart skipped a beat. The last time I'd been there, I'd been riding in a trunk. The Escalade's passenger seat was much more comfortable.

The silence around us was not uncomfortable. We more or less knew what we were doing, and discussing anything else struck me as stupid. Judging by El Príncipe's face, he thought the same thing.

We stayed on Airport for a while and eventually turned left on Webberville. We quickly approached the first light there. Taking a left would lead us to T.B.'s Lounge.

"You said they're at the house behind T.B.'s?"

"Yeah, that's what I heard."

"Cool. Keep your head down. I'll drive by it with my phone in my hand like I'm looking for an address or something. If they're around, we don't want these motherfuckers to see you before we get a chance to surprise them."

Not seeing anything the first time we drove by was not what I had in mind, but El Príncipe's logic was solid. I moved the seat back a bit and then bent forward as much as I could. I looked at the two new dogs on my wrist and prayed for strength.

El Príncipe dug his phone out of his pocket and started messing with it and looking at both sides of the street.

"We're almost at T.B.'s now."

The car slowed down a bit more. I closed my eyes and prayed in silence.

"There's only one small house behind the place. There's no one outside, but there are lights on inside."

El Príncipe kept driving slowly and glancing at his phone. The man was a professional. It almost made me feel bad for criticizing his style. Still, this was only the beginning. I'd heard way too many stories about him kicking doors down and shooting people out in the open in the middle of the day to start thinking he was going to act like a ninja instead of a drunk cowboy the second that cañón he was carrying around came out.

"You can sit up now," he said. "I'm gonna get to the end of the street and turn around. Keep your eyes on the house. See if you can spot anyone inside. Maybe they're not there and just left the lights on."

We turned around. I placed my elbow on the windowsill and covered the lower half of my face with it just in case.

The house was a small brown structure that would look abandoned if you broke one of its windows. The front lawn was a sad mix of dry dirt and yellow grass. The garage door was crooked and missing large chunks of white paint. There were two windows facing the street, both to the left of the garage door. A dark brown door sat between them.

There were no people moving inside the house, but that didn't mean the place was empty.

"Let's park a block or so from T.B.'s and walk back here. We can cut across T.B.'s backyard. There's no fence."

El Príncipe did what I told him.

He turned the lights off and then killed the engine. I looked forward. The few cars in front of T.B.s Lounge meant there wasn't much going on in there. I liked it that way. Less curious assholes once shots started ringing. I hoped that the music inside would be too loud for them to hear and that, if they did, they did the east Austin thing and looked the other way.

"You ready to do this?"

His question came at me like a runaway train and thinking about my answer destroyed that invisible thing that had been holding me together.

The answer was a very loud no, a no yelled at the top of my lungs while running in the opposite direction.

El Príncipe dug into his pocket and pulled out a small vial of blow. He held it in his left hand and unscrewed the top. He dumped some of the white powder on his clenched right fist and snorted it. He passed the vial to me. It'd been a very long time since I'd filled my sinuses with the white fire that comes from la caspa del Diablo.

"Date un pase, cabrón," he said. "Este perico te va a sacar pelo en el pecho y va a hacer que te crezcan los cojones."

The motherfucker smiled at me.

He was wrong. The blow wouldn't make me braver. It wouldn't give me more cojones. However, I knew it would kick whatever Oxy-induced slowness there could be hanging around in my system, so I shook a small mountain onto my fist and snorted it into my right nostril.

Two seconds went by and nothing happened. Then my head exploded.

Snorting shit that's been cut into by greedy hands is one thing, but slapping your brain with pure snow is like dumping your head in cold water and then using jumper cables attached to a car battery as earrings.

"Tengo miedo, güey."

It just came out. El Príncipe looked at me.

"We already talked about this, tipo. We're gonna go see if these motherfuckers are there and take care of business. Vinimos a jalar gatillo y eso es lo que vamos a hacer. You'll be home soon and you'll sleep better knowing no one will be coming for you."

"We're gonna try to use normal bullets to try to kill a man who's really a demonio, carnal. It can't be done."

"Los demonios no existen, papi, sólo están en tu cabeza."

"No, this man is a demonio, he…"

El Príncipe turned to me and slapped my chest with the back of his hand.

"Pull out your gun."

"What? I…"

"Pull out your fucking gun, sácala!" he screamed.

I pulled out my gun. He took it from me and hit me in the head with it. It hurt. A lot.

"You feel that, papi? That's a fucking gun con balas huecas adentro. That's real. Your pain is real. This ain't the time for your religious bullshit. No demons, no saints, no gods, no nothing. We go in there and we kill us some motherfuckers for popping Guillermo and Consuelo. You feel me? This, this shit's real. Get that other nonsense out of your head."

He threw the gun in my lap and got out of the car. I picked up the piece and did the same.

Suddenly we found ourselves standing on the sidewalk, silent and looking at each other.

"Vamos a darle a esto, cabrón."

El Príncipe started walking toward T.B.'s. I followed him. Between his confidence and the blow in my head, I was feeling slightly more confident.

"Vamos a cortar por aquí."

The back of T.B.s was an open space surrounded by trees and dry bamboo. We walked next to the building. Someone was playing blues inside. There was no one smoking out back. We sprinted through the open area and went into the trees.

We approached the back of the small brown house sideways to use the cover provided by the trees and bamboo.

There was a window on the left side. Small. Lights were on behind white blinds.

"Let's walk up to that window, see if we can spot someone or hear anything."

A car drove by. A big brown thing that looked as old as the house. It slowed down. I pulled out my gun. The car kept going down the street. I inhaled.

The window was only about ten feet from us when we heard a laugh coming from somewhere behind it. It was all we needed to hear.

El Príncipe crouched a bit. I did the same. He looked at me.

"These motherfuckers don't know me. We'll go around and I'll knock on the door. You hide next to me. Stay low. I'll pop whoever answers in the face and start shooting at anyone else inside. You'll come in behind me. Try to get next to me if it's clear. Don't shoot from behind me. If you fucking shoot, te juro que te mato."

The plan was crap. It was a suicide mission. It was exactly why I'd told Guillermo not to put El Príncipe on it from the start. Knocking on a door and shooting everyone inside once the door opened didn't even deserve to be called a plan. Not even if I had been smart enough to score a vest. However, I had nothing better, so I went with it and nodded because I was too scared to talk.

We walked slowly, our bodies almost brushing against the side of the house. We were both listening for any kind of sounds coming from the other side of the wall. When we reached the corner of the house, El Príncipe looked at me and nodded. No words. No encouragement. Absolutamente nada.

He walked past the first window without crouching. At some point, he had taken out his massive gun and was now holding it behind his back. We reached the edge of the house and he turned, looked at me with a smile on his face, and nodded. He moved casually forward. I followed at an uncomfortable crouch, staying about five or six feet from him. He reached the door and used his left hand to knock. His knocks sounded like explosions to me.

My breathing was fast and shallow. I was getting dizzy. El miedo me estaba volviendo pendejo. I heard voices inside, one of them approaching the door. There was a click.

The door opened.

El Príncipe raised his gun and fired.

It sounded like the end of the world.

I blinked and he was gone. I stood up and ran to the door.

The guy on the floor only had half a face. The half he still had was covered in tattoos. The puddle of blood was growing fast.

El Príncipe was aiming at a hallway. He squeezed off a second shot. His right arm flew up like the gun wanted to take flight. He held it with both hands. Another explosion rocked the house.

Screams were coming from the rooms in the back of the house.

A figure popped up from behind a ratty brown sofa to the right of the hallway's entrance. Brown dude. Shirtless. Covered in ink. Our guns moved to him simultaneously. My shot got off first, turned into an explosion of dust and plaster. The guy ducked, threw his hands up to cover his head. The second shot came. El Príncipe had actually aimed. The guy's shoulder erupted. Red splattered the wall. The guy looked like a football player had pushed him against the wall. The arm covering his head went down. He kept moving. I squeezed my trigger again. The top of his head vaporized into a cloud of red mist.

Two down. Judging from the voices inside the house, there were more than two to go.

Then someone was shooting at us from the hallway. I dropped to the floor. El Príncipe grabbed his cañón with two hands and squeezed the trigger twice. I could feel each shot deep in my chest the way you feel the bass when the music is too loud at a club.

I half-ran, half-crawled my way to the wall where the dead guy was. My plan was to shoot those pinches culeros from a low angle. Maybe that way would they wouldn't see me coming. I looked at El Príncipe. Bullets were flying out of the darkened hallway like bees from just-kicked nest, but the guy stood there, aiming his gun like he couldn't be touched by bullets. Boom. His cannon exploded again and his arms kicked up. Then a bullet caught him in the chest and he stumbled back. He fired again with one hand. The gun bucked like a pissed off mule. A second later his head snapped back. He dropped back. Didn't move.

I realized I'd have to use my left hand if I wanted to sneak my gun into the hallway and get a few shots off without getting shot in the face.

I'd never shot a gun lefthanded. It felt weird. I pulled the trigger four times. No screams, but the shooting stopped for a few seconds.

A man came running out with something long and black in his arms. He made the mistake of looking right first the second he left the hallway. I lifted my gun and pulled the trigger. He bent over and screamed. He looked at me. From his bent position, he moved the rifle in my direction. I squeezed off two more shots. I don't know where one of them went, but the second turned the left side of his neck into a red mush. La sangre salió disparada como en las películas de Tarantino.

My ears were ringing from the shots and the smell of cordite was raping my nose.

No shots came from the rooms. I sat there and waited, feeling like my heart was trying to kick his way out of my chest.

Then I heard feet.

They were moving away from me. Then there was another sound I didn't recognize. It took every ounce of will I possessed to flatten myself against the floor and take a peek at the hallway.

It was empty.

I'd have to get my ass up and go finish this thing.

I prayed.

Santa Muerte, por favor deja que sólo sean cuatro.

If there was more than one marero in those rooms, I was muerto.

Consuelo. I needed her voice. It didn't come.

I looked down at my arm. The two dogs were still there. She was there.

I stood up and pressed myself against the wall. The ringing was slowly subsiding, but not fast enough. If someone was whispering or moving around in those rooms, I wouldn't be able to hear them.

My eyes went to El Príncipe's body. I thought about grabbing his vest, but moving his body around was a sure way to get killed.

Santa Muerte, protégeme.

I said it out loud. Then I moved into the hallway, my gun leading the way with its dark belly still pregnant with some blessed balas.

The first door was on the left. It was open. Darkness ruled beyond the doorway. The second door and third doors were on the right. The last door had to be the room we'd seen from the back of the house. The light was still on. The door before it had to be the bathroom. It was dark, but enough light from the last room was spilling out for me to make out a white counter.

Indio had to be in that last room.

Consuelo's slashed neck came to me. Her body slumped against the kitchen cabinets like some discarded piece of garbage. I needed the anger to come back and kick the fear out like a tenant who won't pay rent.

Santa Muerte, protégeme.

Short and simple. Un mantra personal e immediato.

Santa Muerte, protégeme.

A breeze came in and caressed my sweaty arms. I thought it was un mensaje divino. I closed my eyes, whispered a thank you. Then the breeze came again.

The window.

Indio was escaping.

I heard laughter coming from behind me. I turned, gun raised. There was no one there. Then the laughter came again, but from behind me.

I ran into the room. There was a mattress on the floor and a few bottles next to it. It smelled like weed smoke and sweat. The window was open. The blinds were moving gently in the breeze. El pinche hijueputa se había fugado. I had to go after him.

I moved to the window, moved the blinds out of the way, and placed my hands on the windowsill so I could lift a leg and jump out.

My right leg touched the grass and something came at me fast. I saw white balls of light all around me.

Indio.

He'd been waiting for me.

The butt of his gun came down on my head again. The balls of light clicked off. My legs bent. My right hand let go of the gun. Indio grabbed the back of my shirt and pulled me the rest of the way out, let go. My body hit the ground. Air left my lungs. Indio growled and kicked me. Something in my chest cracked. It felt like someone had put a blade in me.

"Lo nuestro es matar a bala, marica."

His voice would've made wolves run away.

"Tu no eres nadie, cabrón. Nadie jode con la Salvatrucha. Nadie jode conmigo."

He kicked me again. The knife in my ribs went in deeper. My eyes were open, but all I saw for two seconds was absolute darkness.

Indio's hand was on me again. He pulled me by up by my shirt and screamed something in a strange language. The sound was something physical. It hit me like a gust of hot air. My feet left the ground for a few seconds. His strength wasn't human.

He was angry. Spit was flying out of his mouth. His words ran into each other and became growls. Then he stopped, shoved me down, and stood straight. He threw his head back and started speaking in that bizarre tongue again, but now it sounded like three or four people talking at once.

I looked up. His mouth wasn't moving, but I could still hear him. What looked like tiny hands were pushing against the skin in his stomach from the inside. The skin stretched like a ballon and then retreated. I wanted to scream, but couldn't.

The black eye of Indio's gun was down looking at me.

I wanted to get up, take that gun from him, shove it up his ass, and pull the trigger. I couldn't. Todo lo que podia hacer era sentir dolor. My favorite prayer came to me.

Señora Blanca, Señora Negra, a tus pies me postro para pedirte, para suplicarte, que hagas sentir tu fuerza, tu poder y tu omnipotencia contra los que intenten destruirme.

Before I could continue in my head, Indio spoke. His voice belonged to a monster, but it was loud and clear over the mumbled nonsense of those other voices that were coming from everywhere and nowhere.

"Ogún oko dara obaniché..."

His eyes were filled with blackness. The tiny hands were gone replaced by the outlines of faces. A few flies flew out of his mouth.

"...aguanile ichegún..."

A thin black tube appeared next to Indio's head.

Thup.

His head snapped sideways. The arm holding the gun dropped down. He followed.

A black 9mm was attached to the silencer. Holding both of them and looking down at me was the Russian. He looked at Indio's body, lowered the gun a bit, and put two more bullets in his skull. His eyes were now normal. A few more flies came from his mouth. His stomach and chest no longer moved.

"He bleeds," said the Russian.

I coughed. Grunted from the pain.

"You and your friend are very stupid men, Nando."

I wasn't about to argue with him. He was absolutely right.

"You are lucky that I am curious. You are lucky that running away a second time made me feel bad. You should thank my mother. She talked me into coming here without saying a single word. Pray for her dusha."

I nodded.

"I will get out of here now. Too much noise. Cops will be here soon. I suggest you disappear as well. Don't take that car you came in. Do you need to come with me?"

I nodded again. I wanted to thank him, but words wouldn't come. The Russian reached out to me. I grabbed his hand. He yanked me up as if I weighed nothing. White hot pain flared in my chest. I leaned on him. We started walking.

"The Tchort that was following you, he is dead now."

"He… he is. Thank you."

"This man with the black eyes, I did not kill him for you, Nando, I killed him for me."

That statement didn't require an answer.

We walked around T.B.'s Lounge. The Russian's car was the same big beast I'd seen earlier. He opened the door and helped me get inside. Then he climbed in and we took off. The Russian didn't ask me where I lived.

"Your boss, he is dead. What will you do now?"

"I don't know. I'll figure that out soon, but first I want to buy some apples, take something for the pain, and then pray. I want to pray to mi Santa Muerte for an entire day. Then I might take my neighbor out for some tacos or something. I don't know."

The Russian didn't say anything. He looked at the road ahead of us with eyes that were entirely white.

ABOUT THE AUTHOR:

Gabino Iglesias lives in Austin, TX. This is his second novel.

ACKNOWLEDGEMENTS

I want to thank J David Osborne for believing in my weird words. Working with you is an honor and a pleasure. Much love, hermano. You and Rios son familia.

I want to thank Ady and Gabi, por lo de siempre, por todo.

Rios de la Luz and Steve Lowe looked at chunks of this novel early on and made it better. You two are awesome people, friends, and writers. If anything here is good, it is because of them.

Matthew Revert, where would I be without you? Thanks for everything.

For their friendship, words, and inspiration, big hugs and thanks to Jeremy Robert Johnson, Brian Allen Carr, Bill Minutaglio, Jerry Stahl, and Cody Goodfellow, the fucking madman genius you can blame for that mysterious bucket. Un abrazo enorme para Isaac Kirkman, a visionary man of words who became a part of this in many ways. One of them is the unblinking visionero in this book. Keep the light flowing, street poet.

There's a group of fantastic people who have become a community for me. They keep me inspired and humble, so thanks to Cameron Pierce, Adam Cesare, Michael Kazepis (this book's title? His doing), Michael J. Seidlinger, D. Foy, Constance Ann Fitzgerald, Ryan W. Bradley, Eddy Rathke, Tiffany Scandal, David James Keaton, Carlton Mellick III (I wouldn't be here without you, man), Sean and Jessica Leonard, Noah Cicero, John Skipp, Laura Lee Bahr (squee!), Grant Wamack, Michael Allen Rose, Sauda Namir, Shane Cartledge, Ryan Harding, Joseph Bouthiette Jr., Josh Myers, Jeff Burk, Brian Keene, David Bowles, William Pauley III, Jamie Iredell, Kelby Losack, Dyer Wilk, Brian Allan Ellis, Jim Ruland, and David W. Barbee.

Thanks to the folks who always support what I do in ways that are as undeserved as they are unexpected: Steve "Boo" Pattee, Daniel LaPonsie, Micheal Sean LeSueur, Benoit Lelievre, Vincenzo Bilof, Scott Cole, Tim Marquitz, Adrian Shotbolt, Christoph Paul, Reagan Butcher, and Jackson Ellis, who has made Verbicide feel like home.

Since this is my first "crime" novel, a shout out to Jedidiah Ayres, Nik Korpon, Joe Clifford, Tom Pitts, Anthony Neil Smith, Keith Rawson, Craig T. McNeely, Court Merrigan, Rob Hart, and Paul J. Garth.

Gracias a los amigos de siempre: Trobi, Manu, Gambi, Perla, Willie. Se les quiere, cabrones.

A todos los barrios del mundo y su gente buena. A Mexico, Puerto Rico, Austin, and those who, like me, came to this country to follow a dream. Hope y'all find what you're looking for. And gracias a la Santa Muerte.

Made in United States
Orlando, FL
19 December 2022

27285736R00119